DON'T BREATHE A WORD

DON'T BREATHE A WORD

HOLLY CUPALA

HARPER TEEN

An Imprint of HarperCollinsPublishers

HarperTeen is an imprint of HarperCollins Publishers.

Don't Breathe a Word
Text copyright © 2011 by Holly Cupala

Library of Congress Cataloging-in-Publication Data
Cupala, Holly.
  Don't breathe a word / by Holly Cupala. — 1st ed.
    p. cm.
  Summary: Joy Delamere is suffocating from severe asthma, overpro-
tective parents, and an emotionally-abusive boyfriend when she escapes
to the streets of nearby Seattle and falls in with a "street family" that
teaches her to use a strength she did not know she had.
  ISBN 978-0-06-176669-5
  [1. Self-actualization (Psychology)—Fiction. 2. Homeless
persons—Fiction. 3. Street children—Fiction. 4. Asthma—Fiction.
5. Psychological abuse—Fiction. 6. Family life—Washington—
Seattle—Fiction. 7. Seattle (Wash.)—Fiction.] I. Title. II. Title: Do not
breathe a word.
PZ7.C91747Don 2011   2011009147
[Fic]—dc22   CIP
                                                                    AC

Typography by Ray W. Shappell
12 13 14 15   LP/BV   10 9 8 7 6 5 4 3
❖
First Edition

For my family,
and for Amy, Pam, Deanna, Glynis, Kristine, and Alice—
sisters not by blood, but by choice.

And for Shiraz. Always, always for you.

ACKNOWLEDGMENTS

My deepest gratitude to the many people who helped bring this novel into being:

To Catherine Onder, Sarah Dotts Barley, Tara Weikum, the amazing team at HarperCollins, and my friend and agent Edward Necarsulmer, for their warm support and tremendous contribution to Joy's journey and mine.

To my faithful writer friends for their ideas and insight: Martha Brockenbrough, Janet Lee Carey, Molly Blaisdell, Jolie Stekly, Peggy King Anderson, Katherine Grace Bond, Judy Bodmer, and Dawn Knight; and to readergirlz, for inspiring me with their generous hearts and inviting me to be part of it all.

To librarians, booksellers, bloggers, and YA lovers who

have showered me with support and enthusiasm. I am profoundly grateful for you.

To Jack Brace, who asked us to give backpacks and socks and gave me the flint for this story; to Veronica Bandin for helping me give Santos a voice; to Bo Gilliland for revealing secrets of the Seattle underground music scene; to Gena Garcia for showing me what it's like not to breathe; to Josephine at the bead store for providing invaluable intel on life in Capitol Hill; and to Pam Longston and New Horizons, for bringing truth to Joy's experience and for working so tirelessly to shelter homeless teens.

To Mom, Dad, Ginger, and John for believing in me since day one and being my wonderful family, and to my dear friends who are just like family.

Most of all to Shiraz, Lyra, and the One who brought us together, with love.

DON'T BREATHE A WORD

1

Slyt. Slyt.

Sliding metal cut through the still night, spiraling ribbons of hair into the sink.

But better the sound of scissors than the rattle of my lungs. One wrong breath would set off the alarm.

I scooped up the strands and thrust them into a plastic bag, right next to what was left of the Manic Panic bleach kit and the sack full of dirt from the garden. An unknown girl stared back in my bathroom mirror. Jagged white bob. Pale eyebrows, oddly light against fading summer skin. Black rings around the eyes, transforming her . . . *me* . . . from a suburban girl into a hollowed-out specter.

That's what I'll be, if I'm lucky. Invisible.

And silent. I had to be. There was only one chance for escape.

Headlight beams flashed through my open window, putting me on alert. Earlier today, my mom had asked if I needed some new curtains, with Dad's job and everything going so well. As if new curtains would make me forget this beautiful birdcage, suffocating my beating heart. As if they could keep me, now that I'd come to the edge.

No.

I'd already fallen, and there was no one to catch me. Not here, anyway.

I took a harsh swig of my inhaler and suppressed the cough. As long as I was angry, I wouldn't have to feel afraid.

Even in August, it was cold enough in the middle of the night to pull Asher's flannel close, over the T-shirt and ragged grey PVC pants I found at the thrift store. His smell—hand sanitizer, cigarettes, clean custom scent—still permeated the fibers. I would leave everything else, but at least I'd get the flannel out of the deal.

I ran a tissue across the sink to capture any lingering strands. Who knew what forensics team they might call out when they found me missing? It would be worse than when I'd almost died of pneumonia. The only trail they'd find would be the one carefully laid by me—a scrape of mud, a smudge on the windowsill. No note. No fingerprints.

My eyes scanned the bedroom one last time for anything I might have forgotten. My window was open to the breeze and my bed unmade, as if I were snatched right out of it. The clock read 1:26 a.m. A muddy pair of men's work boots waited next to my old backpack, stuffed with water bottles and Clif Bars and inhalers. I only took a handful of each so they wouldn't notice what was gone.

Those were the things I'd prepared for, but now that I was leaving, the unexpected reached out to hold me back. Not the laptop or the closet brimming with clothes. Not even the cluster of photographs of me with my best friend, Neeta, at mock trials or by the pool. Or me with my two brothers, a trio of J's: Jesse, Joy, and Jonah. I was always crushed between them, as if they could put the air right into my lungs.

They were a collection of poses, like everything else. A smokescreen, veiling the truth.

Then there was the picture of Asher.

Asher stared at me, leaning back, arms crossed, with a look at the same time blank and challenging. The look that made me ache with hot dread.

Neeta couldn't have known why I'd finally given in to a girls-only trip with her. The photos didn't tell the real story. We hadn't talked, really talked, since I'd been with Asher. You can know someone your whole life, and a year later they know nothing about you at all.

"You're different, Joy," Neeta had said on the way back.

Maybe it was because we'd just gone to see the oldest J at college. Maybe it was because I'd left Asher behind.

But when Neeta said it, I had to push back tears.

The me in the photos mocked the one reflected in the mirror: two of us, divided. J2. *Joy.* That name didn't even fit me anymore. I would become someone she could never be.

"Good-bye, Joy," I whispered. "It'll be better out there. I promise."

The new me would not be powerless. The plan would work. It *had* to. No one would believe I could do this—least of all Asher.

I did feel a little bad for what I was about to do to the carpet.

J1 had been out of the house for a year now, his old bedroom an empty cell. He didn't have to watch over me anymore, now that the job belonged to Asher. J3 slumbered like the dead—or at least like an exhausted four-year-old, his breathing even and thick. My parents had nothing to keep them up at night.

Even still, I held my breath against the earthy smell as I put on the work boots and dumped out the bag of dirt, smearing its contents from the window to the bed and wrestling with my pillows. Dirt could trigger an asthma attack, and that would bring my parents flying into the room. I stuffed the boots into the bag, then swiped my feet through the mud to give the illusion of a struggle. I would leave no other trace. Soon, police would be crawling this room for evidence.

And then—

Crunch.

Pain stabbed into my bare arch, and I clutched my foot to keep from crying out—a Lego wagon from J3, which he'd left here to blackmail his way into my room. The crushed driver dangled pitifully. He'd have no one to watch over him once

I was gone. I stuffed the little Lego man into my backpack before he could make me change my mind.

Nobody would be up and about in our neighborhood at this hour, at least in theory. But that didn't mean I wouldn't get caught by some guy up late with his laptop, who happened to see the ghost of a girl in the night. What the neighbors saw and what went on behind closed doors were often two different things in suburban paradise. I should know.

But I didn't when I met Asher. He dazzled me as much as he did everyone else.

To my parents, he was the perfect replacement for my older brother—even better, he could protect me for the rest of my life. From pneumonia, from poverty, from abandonment.

To me, he was an escape from my parents' obsessive worry. That, and he could shatter me and put me back together again with one tender, electrifying breath, leaving me gasping for more. Delicious danger wrapped in a package of utter security.

Except that for everything he gave, there was a price. If Jesse hadn't been at college, if Mom hadn't been consumed with the details of my medicines and schedules, if Dad hadn't been unemployed for six months and Asher hadn't gotten him the job at Valen Ventures . . . maybe someone would have noticed that I'd stopped breathing.

I didn't even notice, until the night we reached the edge.

Neeta and I were home from our trip. I was still reeling

from Jesse's rejection. If I could count on anyone, it would be him. But he slammed the door in my face.

Asher would be angry—that much I *could* count on. But I couldn't have guessed the punishment. He took me to his apartment like he'd always done, only this time there was a candle burning. The calmness in his grey, grey eyes conflicted with the set of his jaw, made even sharper by the flickering light. He drew back the sheets. Something metal gleamed in the candlelight.

I don't care if anyone else knows . . . I only care if you know, Joy.

That night, I sacrificed myself on an altar of skin and ashes. But I wouldn't bow down.

I skimmed the darkness toward the community entrance: elegant by day, spiked by night. My skin pulsed in that secret place, a blistering reminder that everything Asher did—good or bad—was about power.

My parents were always complaining about the Hopkins girls wedging the gate open for their boyfriends. But this new me was counting on it. I would slip through the bars before anyone knew I'd escaped. I didn't dare glance back.

What drew me forward was a glimmering, singular thought. A memory, a promise.

Help was out there, if only I could find him.

2

The twinge in my lungs was the least of my problems as I passed from shadow to shadow. I would have to take a short-cut through the woods to make the two a.m. bus. If I didn't, I was completely screwed. The next one didn't come until dawn.

I tore through the evergreen belt where Jesse and I used to build forts and where I first met Neeta, long before Jonah was even imagined. *J1, J2, J3.*

Jesse left for Western last summer. J1 would be fine without me. Better, even—he said so himself.

J3 would forget me soon enough. What did Mom always say about memories? Mine began when I was five years old. Jonah had one sweet year left.

The dried-out creek at the bottom of the ravine plunged me through more memories, but I would erase them with every gulp of mossy air. The dirty Vans I found at St. Vincent's would leave the trail of some other girl in some other life, and I would vanish in a flutter of dirt and leaves.

1:52 a.m. on my cell phone. I would turn it off as soon as I hit the city. Life would be in a new time zone, synchronized with a different speed of flight.

At 2:02 a.m., Metro Bus 216 rolled up to the Issaquah Transit Center and I flipped up my hoodie, ready for action.

The bus door jiggled open, illuminated by a fluorescent glow. I had a crumpled ticket in my pocket, torn out of my parents' *Eastside Savings* book. I held it out to the driver, who looked like he hadn't eaten anything but greasy drive-thru noodles for a very long time.

Runaway teen, I could see on his face. I wondered if he could see the desperation on mine. *I didn't look too closely, officer. But no, it wasn't this girl. She had blond hair, not long and dark, and the eyes . . . black and empty.*

The driver sniffed impatiently at my outstretched hand. "Just put it in the slot," he sighed. *Stupid suburban kid, doesn't even know how to ride the bus.* How was I going to survive on the street?

The only other passengers were a woman leaning across the handicap seats and a suit guy in the back. I claimed a bench near the middle and curled into a ball around my backpack.

All I had to do was get to Bellevue, where I could wait for

the first Seattle-bound bus. Then it would take another to get to the Capitol Hill neighborhood, where I would disappear into the ample teen homeless population. Until then, I had to blend into the scenery. That wouldn't be too hard. No one I knew rode the bus.

We rumbled away from the Transit Center and onto the highway. I looked out the back window, past the businessman and into the blackness of my receding life.

"Let's go for a drive," Asher had said, just a few days ago.

We didn't talk about what happened the night before. His anger was expended, once I'd fallen asleep at his apartment and spent the night raging with fever and chills. He took care of me and brought me back to life. He bandaged my wounds and took away the hurt. Now we were at the tender point, the part I hungered for. He was always so kind afterward.

But this time, he'd gone so far. My skin throbbed at the memory.

"Where do you want to go?" I asked, once we were settled into his DeLorean, detailed every week to keep it satiny and fingerprint-free. He could have any car he wanted, but he chose one that required constant care. Like me.

He gently lifted the seatbelt away from my hip and offered me my inhaler, then tilted my mouth to his so that I could taste his familiar mix of smoky and sweet. A warm tingle spread through me—even after the last twenty-four hours, he could still have this dizzying effect.

"How about you choose, Joy."

Normally this kind of statement would be a test. If I could navigate the land mines, I wouldn't be punished. Not this time. A couple of crows picking at roadkill shot us curious looks, giving me an eerie chill.

I tucked my head onto the thickness of his shoulder, feeling it soften under my weight. He touched my hair, my shoulder, everywhere but where the pain was, as if soothing me. It was over now, and I wouldn't run off with Neeta again without telling him. It was going to be better . . . he would stay close, watch over me.

If I could walk this balance, everything would go back to the way it was in the beginning.

We passed a Starbucks on the way out of the neighborhood, where I used to go with Neeta. She could be there now with Ellerie and Ari, her new friends since Asher came along. They'd be sipping Frappuccinos, maybe talking about the trip. I hadn't gotten a chance to ask Neeta what she meant, if she saw through it all. *You're different, Joy.*

I couldn't risk running into them with Asher. As long as I stayed away, I could make sense of what had happened, first with my brother and then last night. Seeing Neeta would jeopardize everything. I would crumble with one look, which would only make things worse.

"We could go to the city," I said. "Maybe get something to eat?" Though food was the furthest thing from my mind.

He nodded, tipping his aviator sunglasses down over his

eyes. I let out the air captured in my lungs. It was what he'd wanted all along.

Seattle unfolded before us, the Puget Sound and the mountains and the entire city crammed into the low, wide windshield. The last droplets of summer rain strained to hold on as we sat in silence.

"You haven't talked much since you got back," said Asher. I fingered the Tiffany bracelet he'd given me, the one with the crow dangling from the edge of the plate. It identified me wherever I went, even to the ends of the earth.

"It wasn't a big deal. It's just . . . Neeta and I haven't hung out in a long time, and she thought we could visit Jesse at Western." The truth was, I didn't even know why I was going to see my brother until I got there.

We got off at the Olive exit, taking us into Capitol Hill. As we drove toward Broadway, the landscape changed from shiny to gritty, silk to leather, boutique to clothing exchange. Street parking became dense, and we circled to find a spot.

"I thought you didn't hang out with Neeta anymore," Asher said, with a hint of disdain. It was no secret he didn't like Neeta. The words *annoying* and *know-it-all* came to mind, even if he had only ever treated her with the utmost politesse.

"We're about to start senior year together," I answered. "She thought we should go on a trip." My skin felt like it was on fire, and I shifted for relief.

The DeLorean growled to a stop at Olive and Harvard. Asher opened the winged door and left it up while he came for me, coolly noting the attention it attracted.

"So what did you do there? It had to have been good if you didn't want to tell me about it. A party?" His question skewered me with dead calm.

We joined the stream of pedestrians, dodging students and people talking to themselves, grimy homeless kids who probably hadn't changed clothes in weeks. When my brother still lived at home, he came down here all the time, handing out food and socks. Asher stayed close to protect me from the mumbling, smoking, unpredictable flow, the softness of his hand contradicting his words.

"No, no party," I backpedaled. "We just stopped by to see Jesse, hung out, and came back." Asher waited for more, for the point that would betray me. Usually I didn't see my error until it was too late.

What I couldn't tell him was that Jesse, the brother who always watched out for me, the one who found me when I'd stopped breathing, didn't want to see me. He would feed the homeless and build houses in Mexico, but he'd had enough of me. There would be no help from him.

"Hung out? And you couldn't tell me about that?" Asher and I stopped in front of the Smoke Shop, the only place around here that imported the cigarettes he liked. A group of crows dive-bombed for a bit of french fry left on the street. He watched them with interest.

Air scraped in my throat like shards. I took a slow breath to calm my voice. I wouldn't cry. I fumbled with my inhaler, and he steadied it in my hand.

"Don't," he said, running his finger along the outline of my jaw and tracing up to the corner of my eye. "Just tell me the truth. Why did you take off like that?"

"Asher, I'm sorry, I didn't think—"

"True. You didn't think," he cut me off. Then he smiled, and I couldn't tell if it reached his eyes under the lenses. "I know it was a mistake. I forgive you." He put his lips to mine, reminding me of that thrilling place between love and danger. I could barely feel the pain anymore. "It's just . . . I missed you. I love you, Joy."

Internally, something released. *It wasn't all bad,* I would tell Neeta if I could. Sometimes he was incredibly, incredibly gentle. I loved him, too.

What happened last night would never have to happen again.

"Wait here," he said. "I'll be right back." Asher slipped into the shop and left me alone on the sidewalk. I knew better than to move.

And that's when I saw *him.* The boy.

No, heard him . . .

I'd met him once before, in an alley of shattered glass.

I could see him better this time in the light. He was probably about my age, with dark brown hair hanging in pieces. Eyes a deep blue, skin rough and tan from exposure, body all wiry limbs. *If he stood up,* I thought, *he would be well over six feet tall.*

His soft voice, a strain of guitar music reached out like a hand pulling me into an embrace.

He knows the use of ashes . . . he makes her shine with ashes . . .

The words sent shivers down my spine.

The boy stopped, meeting my eyes with a strange kind of knowing, as if he'd been a part of my whole conversation with Asher. He must have recognized me, too. Maybe he remembered what he'd said to me, the last time we met.

I saw how he treats you. If you ever need help, you know where to find me.

On the ground, the boy seemed . . . safe. Even though the words he had once spoken to me were anything but. I didn't know it then, but those words would change everything.

When Asher came out of the shop, I was still standing there frozen—staring at the boy, our eyes locked with an intimacy both uncomfortable and comforting. Like he *knew* me. Could see right through me.

He could see the wounds, forming scars even now. *Ashes.* The words of his song echoed in my mind.

And I wasn't sure I wanted that kind of knowing. I broke eye contact and darted into the nearest doorway. Asher followed, and we found ourselves in Hot Topic, surrounded by net stockings and studded boots.

"What the hell was that about?" Asher hissed, and I braced myself. Until last night, it was only words.

Mercifully, a boot with four-inch heels distracted him. He ran a finger along them as if he were touching my skin.

"These would look hot on you."

A band tightened around my lungs. Instantly, I hated the boots.

"I want to see you in those." Which, if it had been spoken by someone else, might have been completely sexy. But I knew what it meant with Asher. We would go back to his place, and I would put them on. He would start at my neck and work his way down, always leaving the crow bracelet alone. Would he unwrap the bandage? The thought of it made me hurt.

Through the doorway, strains of guitar music drifted in and curled around me like threads of smoke. Meant to choke me or set me free?

He wishes he could cure the scars . . .

I took out my credit card and gathered the boots. Asher came close enough for me to smell his mint and nicotine. He breathed his soft breath on my neck and his words into my ear: "I don't like what you did last night, Joy. We're going to have to fix it."

That's when I knew there was no way out.

3

My life was broken into three parts: before Asher, after I met him, and after I left.

Everything changed that night last summer, when my mom was down with the flu and my dad took me to the Woodland Park Zoo's fundraiser party instead. My dad still had his job then, culling donations for nonprofit ventures. No one discussed what would happen to me once Jesse left for college.

Even in her weakened state, my mom had given Dad the riot act before we left. *Don't you leave her for one second, Peter. Do you have her emergency inhaler? Are you sure you two will be okay?* No one could forget the ambulance rides, or the times I'd stopped breathing. The fact that I'd almost died—twice—hovered over our family like a dark shadow, and I'd been hospitalized more times than I could count. My dad knew what would happen to him if he didn't bring me home in one piece.

The theme this year was For the Birds, because of the zoo's new pink flamingo exhibit, where a dozen of them slopped around in the muck and dazzled everyone in the drizzly Northwest. The zoo hoped to renovate the penguin exhibit from a fake island to a veritable penguin palace, if only the guests could part with some funds to help out.

I kind of felt sorry for the penguins. They had wings, but they couldn't fly. Tonight, I would be nothing like them. Anything could happen when I felt light as a feather, free as a bird.

The back lawn of the zoo had sprouted a chic village of tents—three full bars, three or four tents with bird-shaped pastries or plumed salmon bruschetta, another one housing silent-auction items, and the big tent: dinner for five hundred, where guests would drool and bid over fabulous prizes to keep those muddy flamingos and penguins afloat.

I wore Neeta's red silk sari, sufficiently birdlike but not over the top. Neeta made me promise not to let anything happen to it, or she'd never let me borrow anything again. The sari top plunged in the front, and I imagined what it would be like if I had an asthma attack and a crew of EMTs had to tear through the beads and delicate silk. I could use a little drama. The thought sent a dangerous thrill through my chest.

Dad and I checked in and each got a paddle with our bidding number—235, the perfect number to represent our family: two parents, three kids, five voices of mayhem and chaos.

"Don't go too crazy," Dad said, "but you can bid in the silent-auction tent."

"What's my limit?"

"Hmmm. How about a hundred? If you want to go over, come find me and we'll discuss it."

I knew "discussing it" would most likely result in a "sure," unless it was totally outrageous. A spa day at the Salish Lodge. Dinner for ten at the top of the Space Needle. Wine collection from Bill Gates. Whatever.

I got drinks for both of us—a gin and tonic for Dad and the featured drink, a Yellow Bird, for myself ("With just the tiniest bit of rum and brandy," the bartender promised me). Dad discussed the finer points of philanthropic fundraising with the VPs and their wives, who all wore pink boas.

It was strange to see them in person, after hearing about all of their secrets—affairs with students; money-laundering charges; children in rehab. Each one of them looked as numb as if they'd taken a shot of Botox to the heart.

"I'm going to check out the silent-auction tent," I whispered as they started an impassioned discussion of fund funneling, or something like that.

Dad surveyed me with concern. "Are you sure?"

"*Dad*. There are a thousand people with cell phones standing around. If I'm about to die, I'm sure one of them can call 9-1-1."

I could tell he was replaying Mom's warnings in his head, but the veeps' conversation pulled him in like a tractor beam. "Just make it back in a half hour for the animal encounter."

Thankfully, we hadn't gone for the flamingo tour and instead opted for feeding the giraffes, one of my favorite zoo activities. At the south end of the park, a handful of them roamed around Seattle's version of Africa. The zoo had planted trees and bushes to look like the real savannah, only they were actually northwest plants that could survive ten months of rain and still feel like home to the animals.

I sipped my mostly–orange juice and started to feel a little tingly. My heels sank into the damp grass with the sound of a kiss.

It was easy to cruise from one silent auction item to the next. A spice collection from Café Shiraz; animal books from a local author; glass earrings for a flowy-linen Grandma type. I stopped at a vintage collection of Kurt Cobain memorabilia from the Experience Music Project archives—a signed first-edition CD, a T-shirt from the early days, a signed picture of Kurt and Courtney. My stomach fluttered a little just looking at it. There were already six bids, up to $540. *Oh well, whatever, nevermind.*

I skimmed along past the manicure packages, the clay elephant sculpture, dinner for two at Coastal Kitchen. If I had someone to take there, I might have bid. It was still well under a hundred dollars for a night of regional food and mystique. The Cranium games caught my attention. Jesse and I could play Hoopla before he took off for Western and I could play Hullabaloo with Jonah, who was about to turn four. I put my number down, 235, and wished I wasn't lost in the three or the five for just one moment.

I sensed a warm presence, and not from the space heater I passed. More like heat mixed with a chill.

His eyes were the first thing that hit me: intense and pale grey, watching me. A dangerous power crackled around him, the force of it nearly burning my skin.

He was trim and rough somehow, though impeccably dressed in a button-down shirt and light pants. His eyes skimmed my body down to the hem of the sari, silky and red around my legs, and I felt the chill again. His hand rested on the Nirvana T-shirt like he already owned it. Then he slipped back into the stream of bodies jostling for space in the tent.

I moved to the other side of the table, feeling those eyes follow me as I went. I stopped at a bracelet with hand-painted saints and looked up. The boy was across the table at the Cranium package, writing down his number. He looked up at me—not quite smile, not quite smirk. I wrote my number down on the saints bracelet. *Take that.*

Moving on to the next row, I couldn't help but peek back. There he was, at the saints bracelet. Memorizing my number? Trying to steal my bid? Well, I wasn't about to lose. I looked around wildly while his back was turned and hit upon—an evening of drinks and music at The Cloud Room. No matter if it was twenty-one and over, somehow I would sneak in with

Neeta and a couple of others, and we'd have a wild night on top of the Camlin Hotel. *235*.

If I was going to lose the Cranium package, I would have to find something for Jonah. A party at Bouncing Castles. Of course. *235*. The boy gave me a dark look while everyone else seemed to be blurring around us.

My knees were shivery where the silk touched them. Every thread seemed to cup my body in the strangest cool-hot way. He wrote his number after mine in a move both infuriating . . . and totally sexy. *101*. One him and one me.

Finally, I bid on a set of handmade tea cozies. That would be the test to separate *coincidence* from *stalker*. Worst-case scenario, I would present them to my mom as a gift for coming to the zoo party in her place. The question now: Would he bid?

I turned the corner on the last row of tables. More art. More dinners. More jewelry than could be worn by a tentful of zoo ladies. He was moving toward the tea cozies, glancing at me and then coolly looking over his shoulder at the hoi polloi, eating, drinking, and being merry. My dress was sticking to me in places where silk should never stick. He reached the tea cozies and squinted at them.

He mulled them over. Flowered. Hand sewn. Flattering for even the fattest tea pot. Machine washable. Really, the ideal gift. He looked up at me, reading the question on my face. By choosing the tea cozies, was he choosing me?

And then, it was over. He dropped the pen. Wrote nothing at the tea cozy stop. He turned and strode out of the tent without a word. I stood alone, only a few feet away from the heater. But I didn't seem to need it anymore as I burned with wonder and humiliation. Was it the tea cozies? Did I make a bad choice? Was I just imagining him following me and maybe even flirting with me? Did I offend him?

I took a gulp of my inhaler.

Someone on a loudspeaker announced the upcoming animal encounter tours, and I broke out of my cocoon of rejection. Dad would be waiting for me, and the only thing I'd managed to place a bid on was a trio of tea cozies. He would question not only my taste but also my sanity.

Our group gathered around the zoo woman holding up a GIRAFFE sign. Each of the wives had a Yellow Bird drink in hand, and they giggled like they may have already had two or three. If my mom were here, I couldn't imagine her joining in. When she wasn't obsessed with the minutiae of meds and refills, she managed accounts for some of the biggest funds in Seattle—she couldn't afford to giggle. I set my Yellow Bird on one of the empty tables.

We were about to head off when *he* appeared—crisp in his white shirt and linen pants but still looking somehow dark, like these clothes weren't the real him any more than my silky red sari was the real me. He spoke to the zoo woman: Could he join our group?

"Asher. Oh, yes. Of course."

Asher. A fitting name. He stood close to me, like we were together. I could smell the faint scent of cigarettes on him.

He was giving me that intense look again—palpable, as if his eyes were somehow capable of sending waves of adrenaline through my body. Fight. Flight. Melt, right there on the zoo path. My dad looked up.

"Asher," he said brightly. "You know my daughter, Joy?"

My dad knew him?

"Actually, yes. We met in the tent a few minutes ago, but I wanted to continue our conversation."

I didn't realize we'd been having one.

4

Thunk.

My head bumped against the bus-stop window for the second—no, third—time since I arrived at the Bellevue transfer
station three hours ago, and I startled awake. Greyish haze lit
the sky uniformly, making it almost impossible to tell whether
today would be cloudy or clear. Cold pricked my skin through
Asher's flannel and the thrift-store hoodie, threadbare and
damp with dew.

The faux-antique clock overhead read 5:23, less than
twenty minutes before the first Seattle-bound bus would lum-
ber past and head into the city with a bellyful of early risers.
I'd only been on this route once, when Neeta's car was getting
leather seats and she, Ellerie, and Ari wanted to go to Nuemos
for a show.

I pulled the hoodie closer around me, straddling the universe of the visible and the invisible. A trickle of courage surged through my veins like the cold air in my lungs.

In a matter of hours, my parents would find my room in chaos. They'd call a state of emergency, not realizing that state had been building for a year. They would comb through the evidence, declare it a kidnapping. They could keep their lives and I could escape mine. To save us all, I would completely disappear.

My parents would call Neeta first, but she wouldn't have anything to tell. Since I'd been with Asher, we'd seen less and less of each other—at first, because I couldn't get enough of him. Later, because he wanted me all to himself.

She'd witnessed the tension between Jesse and me when we went to see him at Western. He opened the door, surprise and then a scowl on his face. But that could mean anything. On the way home, she said I'd changed, though she couldn't say why.

When Neeta didn't have any answers, they'd call Asher.

I only care if you know, Joy.

The memory burned. They didn't know the kind of power Asher had over me in the real world, or the way his words singed even my thoughts. I could only hope the trail I left would be enough.

My phone was in my pocket, though I'd turned it off so no one could track my signal. Stealth research on GPS and cell technology told me that. *Thank you, Wikipedia.*

In the last twenty minutes, commuters had come out of the

woodwork, most of them wearing some variation of the programmer's uniform—khakis and a T-shirt. A woman made a call, looking straight at me. "We have an emergency," she yelled into her phone.

How could she know? Had I ever seen her before? Did she work for Asher's dad? I tried to look away, my heart pounding in my chest. But would she recognize a profile better?

"The McConnell account is in deep doo-doo," she continued, "which means you and I are . . . "

Of course not, I thought. And I was going to have to get over my jumpiness if I was going to make it out here. To become invisible, I would need a power of my own.

When my bus finally reached Capitol Hill, I was starving, cranky, and had to pee. I had plenty of Clif Bars in my stash, which ought to hold me at least a week—maybe two, if I could train myself to need less.

The streets were relatively empty except for the Starbucks on the corner. The aroma of a double-shot skinny latte called to me like a cartoon cloud of temptation. But if I wanted to make the funds last, there were things I would have to give up.

For the last few days, I'd been taking money out of my account a few twenties at a time. Borrowing more from my mom. Raiding my dad's quarter collection. Altogether, I had over two hundred dollars rolled in my backpack, in my shoe, in my pockets. You never knew who might be watching when you pulled out your stash.

The one good thing about buying a latte, though, was the restroom key. Neeta always had to go, so we knew every bathroom on Broadway. The only public one was a tiny metal stall on the street near the Dick's Drive-In, usually smeared with nastiness and toilet paper and littered with needles. At least there was the drugstore—I could only hope they wouldn't remember me.

I peered through the Rite Aid window on the corner of Broadway and Olive. The girl behind the counter couldn't have been much older than me, thick eyeliner rimming her eyes and body straining against the blue store vest, plinking coins into the till. The sign on the door said it would open at seven—nine minutes, according to the flashing First Washington Tech clock. Six fifty-one, sixty-three degrees. It would be a warm day in Seattle.

The bathroom was through the door in the back corner, past a few boxes, and to the right. Neeta and I had been here tons of times on the way to Urban Outfitters, her favorite store. Neeta would buy the cut-out tees, screen-print them with birds and cherries, and wear them with skirts. I would buy the boy shorts, knowing only one person would see them besides me.

I remembered the last time we'd gone there—Neeta and I were looking for Asher's Christmas present, one of the few times we'd been out since I started seeing him.

"Do you think he'd like this one?" Neeta had said, holding up an ancient-looking leather jacket with crackling brown texture.

She was trying, I knew. But she didn't know what Asher could be like. He was brutal about things not fitting into his aesthetic. My clothes, for instance. In the six months since we'd been dating, the color had drained from my wardrobe. Shapes went from loose to sleek, even though I was always pulling at my hemlines—alien to me but beautiful to him. It had gotten even worse since my dad started working at Valen.

"He's not going to like it," I said.

Neeta sighed. "Well, what *is* he going to like?"

"Forget it," I said, then smiled like an offering. "He's impossible. We should just go to Trophy Cupcakes and be done with it. I'll find something for him later."

"You sure?" I could tell she was teetering. The force of cupcakes was strong with this one.

"Yeah," I said. "I'm sure."

In the end, I gave him the latest cell phone from one of my mom's clients.

"Ah. Personal," he said, then handed me a tiny box, the exact shade of Tiffany blue that could be mistaken for nothing else.

I opened the box carefully, cautiously. It was too big to be a ring box, too small to be a porcelain vase or lamp. It was exactly the right size for an ID bracelet, white gold, its flat plate engraved with his pet name for me. *Little bird*. A charm dangled from the side, a bird with red ruby eyes. When I looked closer, it was unmistakably a crow.

"Charm bracelets originated with the ancient Egyptians," he said. "They acted as identification to the gods of the underworld—who you were, your status, who you belonged to . . ."

I stared at the bracelet, a half-smile frozen on my face. Everything Asher did had a meaning. This was his way of marking me. If it hadn't been smooth metal, I would suspect it had a homing signal so he'd always know where to find me.

The bracelet still jangled on my wrist, tucked up under my sleeve. If I'd left it, they would know immediately. I never took the bracelet off, even to sleep. I would have to escape its hold some other way.

A bird's savage caw startled me. The Rite Aid girl finished putting the money into the register and came to unlock the glass doors. She watched as I entered and made my way past the row of candy bars, magazines, and makeup. I looked over my shoulder to see her eyes follow me while she spoke into the phone in a low voice. Whatever. I wouldn't take long. I turned back around and nearly collided with a blue-vested chest.

"What do you think you're doing in here?" It was a tall, balding man in his forties who looked like he might play Scrabble when he wasn't harassing teens.

"I uh . . . uh . . ."

"Well?"

"I just . . . had to use the bathroom." *What does anybody do in a Rite Aid?*

29

"Right," he said. "After you pocket some Max Factor and cough syrup."

"Huh?" I backed away.

"What have you got in your backpack?" He started to reach for me.

"Hey! Don't touch me!" I spun around, and the girl was reaching for the phone again. Were they calling the police on me? "You don't have to—I'm not doing anything, I swear!"

Mr. Scrabble Bouncer was still coming after me, towering over me like a shadow. "No, you're not doing anything, because you're going to *leave*." I bumped into a tangle of bells at the door and practically fell through it. "And tell your friends to quit coming in and stealing everything!"

When I was back on the street again, my hands were shaking and my bladder near bursting. If I was addicted to anything, it was my stupid water bottle.

Starbucks, Neeta would say, *you're my only hope.*

I trudged back to the café. I could swallow my pride. I could ask for the key and hope for the best.

The place spilled out with students and hipsters with laptops, crushing into the communal warmth and smell of roasted coffee beans.

I stood in line sandwiched between a guy texting and a woman listening to voice mail with a scowl on her face. Everyone in the café seemed to be umbilically connected to some form of technology. The hum was more from the collective tapping of keys than from any kind of verbal communication.

When I got to the counter, the barista gave me the once-over—appreciatively, I thought. He was tallish and golden brown, with auburn hair flying every which way and matching the frayed shirt on his narrow frame. He looked like an art student, maybe, over at Cornish. His name tag, slightly askew, read BACH.

"What can I get for you?"

"Uh . . . just the bathroom key."

His face darkened, a weird contrast to his Adam's apple as it bobbed up and down. "Oh. You're one of those."

"Wait," I stammered, mentally counting my change. "I'll get something when I come out." What did J1 say a homeless person could live on? A dollar a day, if I'm careful? And I'd be blowing three-fifty on a clean bathroom?

"Look," he said in a slightly louder voice, "restrooms are for customers only." But he slid the key in my direction. "Just no shooting up in there, okay?" he whispered. "You'll get me fired." To the girl steaming the milk, he said, "Single tall latte, shot of almond."

So he was telling me to shoot almond and not something else.

"Thanks," I muttered, and slipped away with a key and almond anticipation. I could do this, if I had allies.

I thought of the boy I'd seen on Capitol Hill, of his music piercing me to the heart.

If anyone could help me, it would be him.

5

I wanted to continue our conversation, Asher had said that warm summer evening we met at the zoo. I didn't know then how the conversation would end.

The zoo lady and the veeps and the wives in pink boas didn't register the silent transaction that took place between my dad and Asher. My dad had nodded, and in that moment, he gave Asher permission.

Dad turned toward his colleagues, who were ready and excited to feed the giraffes. And I was, too, up until a moment ago. Butterflies, like the ones in the exhibit, expanded in my stomach. Asher stood only a few inches away, but it felt like he'd already burned into my bloodstream, past any defenses I could put up. How could he already know how to unbalance me?

As the group followed the path to the savannah, a murder of crows bolted up in a terrorized mass, squawking and cawing their indignation.

"Filthy, dumb creatures," I muttered under my breath. That's why we were here—to save a bunch of mucky birds. But maybe I had them to thank for Asher's nearness. I could sense the blood in his veins.

"Actually," he replied, "crows are quite intelligent. Almost as intelligent as humans." A couple of the wives clinked their Yellow Birds up ahead, their laughter ending in an abrupt snort. They left a trail of pink feathers in their wake. "Maybe even more, in some cases."

"Really."

"Yes. As a matter of fact, there are a couple of corvid researchers at the University of Washington who tagged a flock a number of years ago." He gave me an intense look, as though I should be impressed.

"So . . . ?"

"So the tagged birds are all dead now, but their descendants still dive-bomb the researchers whenever they walk around the campus. They have to go out in disguise." He crossed his arms. "Pretty impressive for a species of filthy birds."

I needed to come up with something to prove my superiority over the animals, but nothing was coming. The birds were a test. By my silence, I would fail.

"So how do you know so much about . . . what did you call them? Corvids? Are those crows?"

"Crows, ravens—they're both in the corvid family." The intensity of his gaze shifted back a few notches, withdrawing from the thrilling and uncomfortable place it had been. I felt the void. I wanted to impress him, to make him go deeper. But I had no idea how.

"So you know about corvids. Tell me about them." We were falling further and further behind the tipsy group, alone on the jungle path.

He gave me the same half smile, the one where I couldn't tell if he was making fun of me or sharing the joke. Overhead, a sheet of clouds reflected the fading light. The glow sent his face even further into the shadows.

"Well, you could say they're a lot more like humans than most people give them credit for. Or at least, like a certain segment of humans. Teenage girls, for instance."

Again, I wasn't sure—was I sharing the joke? Or was I the butt of it? His eyes blazed. I couldn't get over how my stomach was riding a mysterious roller coaster with which I was totally unfamiliar.

There was something about him. I wanted to know what he thought of me, and if he realized how his proximity made me feel utterly defenseless.

We curved around the path until my eyes landed on painted footprints—gazelles? Wolves? Little yellow footprints led us to the African village overlooking the savannah. The park was completely silent except for a few random animal cries.

"It's only a bit farther to the feeding area," he said. What kind of authority did he have here, that the zookeepers and even my dad knew his name? How old was he? Not a teenager, I guessed. He looked like he could be at least twenty. If he knew my father, maybe he knew about me. Did he know I was only fifteen and would be jailbait for the next two months?

If he noticed my trembling, he didn't show it. His presence made me feel exposed and exhilarated at the same time. What was it about crows that reminded him of teenage girls? The squawking? I wasn't much of a squawker, unless I was coughing. But I hardly had a chance to breathe, with my family watching over me like hawks all the time.

A shortcut through the bamboo trees thrust us back into the group, gathered around a high iron fence. Beyond it, the savannah spread out into rolling hills and waterholes.

My dad carried on a conversation with his boss in the background while the zookeeper explained the feeding habits of giraffes. The women waved branches full of leaves. Two animals came forward—the biggest one could easily reach a second-story window. The sheen of his fur rippled over his muscles, embedded with obvious power. From afar, they looked like such gentle creatures. But they could break a predator in two with one sharp kick.

A second giraffe, quite a bit smaller, came up to Asher's branch, poised to flee. A few feet away, one of the wives laughed loudly when the big giraffe yanked her branch, and the smaller one stepped away.

"Come here, boy," Asher said in a low voice. "It's okay.

She doesn't want to hurt you, big guy. She's just a noisy idiot. Totally harmless."

Asher held out his hand to me. "Come here. Try it. In a minute or two, we'll have an even better chance."

As I held up the leaves, another spotted head popped over the curve of the hill. Voices fell into a hush: *the pregnant one.*

Asher stood so close I could feel his breath trailing down my neck and sending a rush through my nerves. I glanced at Dad to see if he noticed. He smiled and nodded, still discussing the finer points of nonprofits. Either he was paying absolutely no attention, or Asher had some kind of power over him as well.

Tentatively, the pregnant giraffe stepped forward. Soon we could see her neck rising over the crest of the hill, then her body, lean but bulging. We all held our breaths to see what she would do.

"Come on, baby," Asher whispered. Even the flock of wives held themselves together as Asher picked up another branch and dangled it over the fence.

The tipsy wife set down her Yellow Bird drink on the pavement, then waved a new bunch of leaves at the biggest giraffe. He expertly plucked and shirred leaf by leaf, oblivious to what held the rest of us entranced: the mother giraffe, tiptoeing down the hill—sniffing the air, tantalized by the branches in Asher's hands.

Then, all at once, the big giraffe lunged and the tipsy wife shrieked, knocking her drink over and breaking the glass. The sudden explosion sent the mother giraffe away at a gallop.

Asher lay down the branch in a swift, deliberate motion.

"Oh my gosh, oh my gosh," the woman was saying. "I thought he was about to bite off my finger . . ."

Asher shot her a murderous look.

"Well, that's over," he said to me under his breath. "Maybe I need to reassess my opinion of crow behavior—maybe it's less like teenage girls and more like corporate wives." Then, the half smile again.

And this time, I knew he meant for me to share it.

Asher disappeared into the crowd after we came back from the animal encounter. The silent auctions were now closed. I'd never had a chance to outbid him. After I saw him with the giraffes, Asher struck me as the kind of guy who didn't like to lose. Well, at least I would have a trio of tea cozies to show for my night out with Dad.

We threaded our way through the dinner tent to our table, only a few feet from center stage. This year's thirty biggest prizes were listed in the auction book—dinner for ten with the orangutans, a Halloween party at the indoor playground, and the big one, a private jet for twelve to Lake Powell with a week on the sparkling blue waters. I craned my neck to find Asher. I couldn't forget the strength of his gaze, or his gentleness with the animals, or his breath on my neck. Or the fire when his plans were thwarted.

The rest of the table trickled in with fresh Yellow Birds, even the woman who knocked hers over. She'd been forgiven, the giraffe forgotten.

Dinner was a four-course affair—made even more exciting because I wasn't suffocated with the boys and their testosterone. Mom and I were the only ones who even considered basic things . . . like salad.

Here at the zoo, salad was raised to an art form. A crisp head of endive had been sliced into a green coil and sprinkled with squash blossoms, a little green frond poking up like a bird's feather.

When the sommelier came around with the wine, Dad ordered both red and white and slid the white over to me. "Shhh," he said, "just don't tell your mother," and gave me a wink.

The zoo chefs were too classy to serve something in the poultry category, so our choices were lemon-thyme lamb skewers, cedar-roasted salmon, or the vegetarian option I chose: truffles roasted with brie, honey, and figs. Even the birds couldn't object to that.

By the time we got to our choice of blackberry ice cream, flourless chocolate cake, or my favorite, crème brûlée, I'd almost forgotten about looking for Asher. Almost. The wine flowed to my bones and made them feel a tiny bit rubbery. My lips and tongue wouldn't quite behave when I asked my dad,

"So, how do you know that Asher guy?"

Dad smirked and slid the wineglass away from me. "Let's just say his dad has his fingers in a lot of financial pies, including this fundraiser. Steven Valen? Valen Ventures?"

I held back a little gasp. Even I'd heard of Steven Valen, local bazillionaire, known as a brilliant entrepreneur to his friends and a cutthroat tyrant to his enemies.

My dad went on, not seeming to notice my surprise. He was used to handling people with money every day. "Asher has been around this zoo for most of his life. He's graduating early from View Ridge Prep and doing animal research at the U before applying to the Ivies."

"Crows," I said, remembering our conversation alone on the path.

"Yes. He's an unofficial assistant to the corvid—crows, ravens—"

"Right, Dad, I know—"

"Oh. Well, corvid researchers at the UW. You know they get—"

"Dive-bombed," I finished, "every time they walk across campus. I know, Dad. He told me all about it."

"Then he must have also told you they have an extraordinary social hierarchy. Those birds can be quite brutal."

"Yeah," I said, and took a bite of my crème brûlée.

The lights dimmed as a commotion onstage caught everyone's attention—a highly blond, be-glittered couple made their way to the stage and introduced themselves as co-emcees.

Dad leaned over and whispered, "These two are here every year—wait until you hear this guy's auction call."

I settled down into the warm-and-tinglyness of the chardonnay and introductions of the famous people and the big investors. "That's Asher's dad," mine whispered when the spotlight lit up a table on the other side of the stage. The mythic Steven Valen looked kind of basic, actually. Just an older guy with neatly trimmed hair and wire-rimmed glasses, but I could see the same vivid intensity I'd felt from Asher.

And there he was. Not alone. A girl with rippling hair and movie-star cheekbones sat next to him, the two of them laughing at some private joke and his dad looking decidedly annoyed. Asher caught me looking and stared for a moment, then turned his attention back to the girl.

The emcees went on about last year's auction winners, the Seahawks guy in the audience, and the school band itching to perform for us. Then the auctioneer fell into a rhythm all about product number one, then ten, then eighteen in an endless stream of *blah-blahdy-blah a-hundred-dollars-more, a-hundred-dollars-more!* And all that time I couldn't stop thinking about the heat Asher sent though me . . . or the way he demolished me in one brief glance.

It was dark when the dinner and auction finished. Everyone made their way across the green to the silent-auction tent, where zoo staff doled out items.

"Did you get something?" my dad asked.

"Uh, yeah. A present for Mom."

"That was nice." He stopped to dig in his wallet for the credit card. "Here, you can take this." He wiped away the hair from my forehead like he only just realized how mad Mom would be if she knew how much freedom he'd given me. "Are you okay? Do you need help carrying anything?"

I shook my head. I could probably manage the tea cozies by myself. But I took a couple of quick puffs of my inhaler and held back a cough.

I stood in line with my arms wrapped around me. The chardonnay warmth had almost worn off by now, so I was left with only the chill. People were still laughing and talking, even though the flow of Yellow Birds had stopped long ago. Now they would be able to fund not only the flamingos' mud hole but also the new penguin habitat. We had done our duty as good citizens and could go home with full stomachs and happy hearts.

Asher wasn't anywhere among the lurkers waiting for loot. He knew my dad, so he could contact me if he wanted to— if he wasn't already with that blond girl at his table. Maybe he knew I was fifteen and was just playing with me. Maybe I should concentrate on junior year coming up and all the credits I would need to get in to a decent school—attending the zoo fundraiser might even count toward community service.

I handed my number over to the woman at the counter: 235, good for a set of tea cozies.

"Here you are," the zoo lady said, handing me a paper bag with my consolation prize nestled inside. Mom would love them. Or, more likely, she'd re-gift them to the cleaning lady. Oh, well. At least *someone* would love the flowery design.

I hugged the bag to my chest and spun around. And there was Asher, holding a paper bag in each hand. *My* items.

"Well, I hope you enjoy them," I said, a slight slur in my voice, as I moved to stalk past him.

"Wait. Joy." The way he said my name—gravely, but with the same touch of gentleness I'd seen when he fed the giraffes—stopped me. Like we were the only two people in the universe, and everyone else was just fading in the space around us.

"What?" I sputtered. It came out more like a whisper. *Damn.* My voice would betray everything.

"These are for you," he whispered back. I could imagine what those lips would feel like, after the thrill of hearing them say my name. He held out the two bags. "And something extra," he took a step toward me, "though I saved part of it for myself . . ." Our hands brushed as I took the handles. ". . . Because I didn't think it would fit you." His right hand slipped between my arm and ribs and slid all the way down to my hip.

I opened my mouth, but nothing came out. He held up the vintage Nirvana T-shirt. "Oh, well, whatever. *Never*—"

And then his lips met mine so softly that my words still hung between us. I could taste the smokiness of his mouth and chocolate honey on his tongue. Shivers spread over my body, to the tips of my fingers and toes and back.

"See you around," he said. I had to wait a minute to catch my breath. Inside the bags were everything—the Cranium set, the saints bracelet, a party at Bouncing Castles. The signed *Nevermind* album, the picture of Kurt and Courtney, and an envelope for a night out at The Cloud Room with a phone number written in crisp handwriting: "Call me."

Apparently, I had a date.

7

Thinking about that kiss now left a bad taste in my mouth, made worse by the lingering effects of coffee on an empty stomach. I finished the last dregs of the latte and tossed the cup into a trash bin.

All right, Capitol Hill. Time to wake up.

Right about now, J3 would make a path through his Legos and Brio trains and trudge down the white stairs, looking for cereal. My mom would be lining up lunches, meds, and keys before going to work—anything to give the illusion of control. Dad wouldn't be far behind. On the way out, he might notice somebody forgot to set the alarm. The cleaning lady would come at noon, when she'd see the dirt on the carpet and the open window. Maybe she wouldn't think anything of it. Mom and Dad would get home around seven and assume I was with Asher. At ten, they might start to worry. Eventually Dad might call the cleaning lady and find out about the dirt, all the evidence sucked up by a vacuum cleaner . . .

That's when all hell would break loose.

The rest I didn't want to imagine. There would be fallout. My parents would be frantic and Jonah would be frightened. I knew I was leaving a nightmare in my wake . . . the thought of it made my lungs hurt. I focused on the things I knew: I needed a place to sleep. I needed to find the one I was looking for. I needed to never look back.

Churches and shelters were off limits. Then there were places I had been with Asher, or with my friends. Any of those could give me away. Instead, I would cross from one world into another, where the weak became strong.

I would need to be strong if I was going to make it out here. Superpowers would come in handy, but I would settle for street powers. My street power would be invisibility. I would hide in plain sight.

Though I doubted anyone would recognize me, with twenty inches of never-dyed hair gone. I pulled the envelope addressed to Locks of Love out of my backpack. A page of stamps had to be enough to send a pound of dark hair from an anonymous Seattle mailbox. I felt strange without it—light. Unencumbered.

My reflection in the bathroom shocked even me—hair a cottony white, bleached as white as two lightening kits could get it. Eyes rimmed black, smudged by my nap on the bus.

Even the one person I wanted to recognize me wouldn't know me now. I thought of his voice, following me even after I had ducked away from his gaze into Hot Topic—penetrating and intimate. Not like Asher, who made me feel stripped and vulnerable every time he looked at me. This boy, whoever he was, made me feel vulnerable in an entirely different way. If he had a street power, it was music. It spoke to my soul.

I knew it was crazy to think he could help me, this boy with the guitar whose name I didn't even know—only the eyes that met mine, promising his help.

When I called Asher after the zoo party, I didn't know I would be trading one prison for another. I only knew I was suffocating.

Not in the literal sense—my family made sure of that. Ever since I almost died from pneumonia when I was five, they watched over me with the kind of attention you'd give to an abandoned baby bird.

I'd been in and out of hospitals countless times with pneumonia and asthma attacks and another near-death experience at age nine.

We all knew the drill. One stray molecule of mold or dust would send me into a fatal spiral, so when my mom wasn't working, she spent the rest of her waking hours making sure every speck of air in the house was vaporized and nebulized and sanitized. The cleaning lady came so often that one time

Jonah called her *Mama*.

No one said anything, because everyone knew the sacrifices we had to make.

Jesse did, all too well. Before he left for Western, his job was to keep me from dying—first by watching out for me on the playground and later by driving me to and from appointments, drugstores, and classes. I couldn't really blame him for wanting to escape. Sometimes I felt so trapped, I wished I'd just stop breathing.

That is, until I met Asher. I didn't know how someone so measured, so deliberate, could make me feel on edge and out of control. I longed for things to be out of control for once in my life.

I called the number he'd given me. He seemed distracted, like he couldn't quite remember who I was.

"We met at the zoo party," I said, slightly incredulous. Did he meet and kiss and buy bags of Nirvana stuff for so many girls that he couldn't remember who I was? "Joy," I said. "Joy Delamere."

"Joy," he repeated, this time with an intimacy that shocked me. He could do that—go from cold and distant to inside my skin in an instant. I regretted my angry tone.

"Sorry, I was working on something," he said, the heat back in his voice, like the grey smolder of his gaze at the zoo. "So you were calling to ask me to The Cloud Room."

I laughed. I hadn't ever met anyone so confident, so quick to unhinge me with his boldness. "Well, yeah. I guess so."

"You didn't come across as a girl who guesses," he said. "You seemed pretty sure of what you wanted at the zoo party. And . . . here I am. So, ask me."

I didn't see myself that way—I was the girl caught between two brothers, at the mercy of one wrong breath. The fact that he saw me as sure of myself sent a ripple of pleasure through my skin.

"So," I said. "I have this gift certificate someone gave me for The Cloud Room. It's for four, so I was thinking—"

"Ah," he warned, and I remembered the flash of fire. Hot. Very hot. A girl could be consumed in that kind of fire.

"I was thinking," I began again, "maybe the two of us could go . . . "

"Mmmm," he murmured. Approval.

" . . . and then, maybe we could go again another time . . . " I waited for his voice to cut through the static. It was hard to guess at what he was thinking when I couldn't see his face.

"Hmmm," he said, as if considering my proposal. "Interesting idea. Why don't we try once, and see how it goes."

A week later, we were on the roof of the Camlin, me with my fake ID and Asher inspecting it for flaws. He told me more about his work with crows, like the vending-machine project. The crows came to it for treats, then learned they could put coins in the slot for more. Eventually, the crows learned to scavenge for change in order to keep the treats coming. The project practically paid for itself.

"People are no different. It's extraordinary what they will

do for rewards—over time, you can give them less and less. You can even introduce punishment, but they'll keep coming back."

The comparison of crows to people made me uncomfortable. "Are you going to study zoology?" I asked.

"Of course not. I'm preparing for politics and psychology."

"But I thought . . ."

He kissed me gently, and I had to catch my breath at the spark that passed between our lips. "Let me explain. If you can learn to manipulate the social hierarchies of animals, the natural next step is people. They aren't all that hard to control."

I blinked, feeling for a moment the power he already had over me. It rushed through me like lightning.

This was the beginning of my dance with fire—the heat, the burning, the pleasure of him going deep into me, trying me, testing me, pulling and pushing and molding and shaping me into the other half of him, distant and cold in some moments and shocking me with his force at others. And just when I was finished, tired of being pushed away and then reeled back into the sheer consumption of it, he would do something so amazingly tender that I would forget what made me want to leave him. Because there, at his apartment, in his car, in his arms, we were two, only two, and I was the most important thing in his universe—not the girl crushed by her parents' constant worry but the center of someone's passion.

My parents knew Asher's parents. They knew of Asher's work and reputation. He would finish out his last year at View

Ridge Prep while I was a junior at Eastside, then he'd take a year to do crow research before heading to an Ivy. He was a good boyfriend for me, the perfect guardian now that Jesse was gone. They knew nothing of the fire that drew me to him, dangerous and alluring.

Everything changed when my dad lost his job. Even more, my relationship with Asher changed.

Dad came home one day and told us all it was over. "People just aren't investing in nonprofits these days—not like they used to. It's a tough economy." They were "reducing expenditures," and my dad was the first one to go.

When I told Asher, he nodded, like he'd known all along. "Yeah. I've heard there was some insider stuff going on."

"What do you mean?"

Asher gave me a smile, patted me on the knee. "Don't worry about it."

But I did worry about it as things got tighter at home. Days stretched into weeks and months, living on Mom's part-time salary while Dad job searched.

Then Mom's hours were cut back. We were about to lose the house, school, medical insurance. All of this while Asher's family empire seemed to be expanding and even profiting from the growing recession.

Dad sank into a depression of his own.

Mom started looking at apartments.

I was the one who could save us—by asking Asher for help.

"What do you want me to do?" Asher had demanded, and

I asked him. Could he get my dad a job?

A week later, Dad had an interview and Asher took me back to his apartment.

It was my first time, with him or anyone else. He kissed the places where my clothes had been, and I was afraid but grateful. I owed him this much.

He agreed.

8

Capitol Hill was almost unrecognizable by day. The axis of Broadway and Pine meant boarded-up clubs, a college, restaurants, and a spider's network of dilapidated businesses. I had only one thought on my mind: finding a place to crash. An empty house? A dryer vent? Just someplace safe for tonight.

There were always plenty of grubby people scattered along Broadway, playing guitars or singing or acting out strange, senseless monologues, asking for spare change. *Spainging*, my brother Jesse called it. He knew the homeless scene well, after all of his volunteering. I bet he never guessed his sister would be one of them.

When I came up here with Asher, we followed the unspoken rule: Never make eye contact. That was as good as telling them you had money to give.

Now they had the power, and I had none. Nowhere to sleep. Nothing to eat except for the emergency rations in my backpack. I hugged it closer and scurried past the lineup of kids sharing a light and the men whose odor and hunger were almost tangible. Other people walked past as if they were invisible. *We* were invisible.

"You're new here." A gaunt, bald man—all leathery skin and whiskers and smelling like he slept in a sewer—blocked my path. I tried to walk around him.

"Hey." His voice slammed hard as a brick. "I'm talking to you."

Only yesterday, I would have been as hidden to him as he was to me, protected by an unseen armor. Suddenly, I was more vulnerable than I was standing naked in front of Asher.

"Hey, are you deaf, little girl?" The man reached for me, and I darted out of his path. His filthy hand landed on my shoulder and brushed my backpack. The others watched, waiting to see what would happen. One of them, a big boy in chains with his hair shaved into a black mohawk, took a drag on his cigarette. He watched me with a mixture of fascination and hate. The girl next to him wouldn't meet my eyes.

"Leave me alone," I mumbled, and backtracked. Up ahead was the hospital, the Garage, Atlas Clothing: areas I knew, when I was Joy. Behind me: Safeway, Urban Outfitters, the Rite Aid that kicked me out this morning. Starbucks, where the guy named Bach might still be working. This scary guy wouldn't mess with Starbucks. They'd call the police, but would someone call the police for me?

Something tripped me—the mohawk boy with the mean eyes—and I stumbled forward. "Better go home," he said under his breath.

I started walking fast toward Urban Outfitters. The old guy followed at a slow, menacing pace, his stench blowing toward me and filling my nostrils with fear. The light turned red, but I didn't stop. A long horn sounded only a few feet behind me. Two students stood at the corner, looking over and then turning away as I approached. Invisible—exactly as I wished.

I looked over my shoulder and he was still there, waiting at the light while a police car cruised past. I hid my face. They could be looking for me by now. If I hadn't done a good enough job with the dirt . . . if Jonah had snuck into my bedroom for a wake-up hug . . . if my mom checked my bed to see what I was doing today . . . Pictures of me could already be transmitted to every police BlackBerry. Every cop in the city could be looking for me, yet they wouldn't see the chase right under their noses.

I reached the Urban Outfitters on the corner of Harrison and Broadway. There were the couches and shabby-chic housewares in the front, then racks of fall dresses and fluttery shirts and cardigans. I slipped inside, hoping to lose scary Stench man here in the retail maze.

I could call Asher now, I thought, tucking myself between two racks of jeans. He could come get me and take me home, and I could explain everything as just a big misunderstanding. He would be angry, and he'd know I wasn't telling the truth, but I'd stick to my story as if my life depended on it. All I had to do was turn on my phone.

My stomach growled, as much from hunger as from adrenaline. The bells on the door jingled wildly. Was that Stench? Would he actually follow me into a store?

I ducked further down past the jeans. I could make it out the back door into the shopping center, but I had an even better chance if I could get to men's clothes.

In the center of the store a metal staircase swept up to the second floor—I would have to cross a wide expanse to get there. I bent down to look for his feet, which would be filthy and ragged. My face was so close to the ground, I could feel the hum of passing traffic. Jeans and dresses obscured my view. Then two tiny, vintage boots appeared, attached to a short girl with a ratted-out brown updo. She looked too nice to be angry, and yet her eyebrows were knitted in a combination of rage and fear. Of me? Or was Stench right behind her?

"What are you doing down there?" she demanded. I tried to stay down, to indicate the urgency of silence. Every word she spoke endangered my life.

She let out an annoyed huff. "What's going on?" She started to reach for the walkie-talkie at her hip.

"No, wait," I said, as an acrid smell hit my nose. She made a face and turned around.

"Hey!" she said with a surprising amount of authority. "You're not supposed to be in here," she said to Stench and brought the walkie-talkie to her mouth. "Security!" she called in a bored tone.

Now was my chance. I could dart behind the stairs to the atrium. The drugstore in the basement had to have a back door, or at least a bathroom where I could figure out what to do next.

I made a move and Stench followed, but by then a couple of security dudes were pounding down the stairs and taking him by the shoulder.

"I was just looking for somebody," he groused.

"Riiiight, buddy. Why don't you go back outside, or you'll be spending the night in jail." One of the guards held his walkie-talkie to his mouth, ready to say the word.

"I'm not the one you should be looking for. She'll steal you blind!" I heard him shout, but I had already slipped out the door, clutching my backpack and veering toward the other end of the mall. The smell of samosas hit my nose from the Indian food cart, reminding me how hungry I was, but I couldn't afford to stop. I wound my way through the atrium to the opposite street corner and ran past another lineup of panhandlers. None of them was the boy with the guitar, the only one I'd trust to help me.

Where was he? He would be hard to miss in this crowd. Was I crazy to think I could find him?

I dodged down a side street further up Broadway and landed

at the Daughters of the American Revolution property—a house from 1900-something, restored and repurposed into a historic reception hall. A row of camellia bushes bordered the west side, big and shadowy enough to hide one small, white-haired girl. I folded myself into the space underneath, taking two deep breaths with my emergency inhaler and willing my heart and lungs to calm down. Voices drifted from the first-floor window, a gentle murmur. If Stench tracked me here, at least they would hear my scream.

But he didn't come.

My phone poked into my hip as I stripped the packaging off of the Clif Bar. It was maybe two in the afternoon, and I still hadn't figured out where to sleep. Maybe here, if I could camp out for a while. J1 had told me homeless people mostly slept during the day and stayed awake at night. Now I understood why.

I could go back now and no one would be the wiser, except for my strange new look. Asher might like it. He might even laugh when he figured out what had happened. *You couldn't even last a day without me,* he would say. And then the real punishment would begin.

I couldn't imagine what could be worse than what happened that night, but I was sure Asher could.

The crow bracelet jingled on my wrist, where he'd tagged me just like those professors tagged the flock of crows.

I don't like what you did last night, Joy . . .

But I would be different now. I would show him this was

no game. I could leave everything behind, including the words he tossed like poisoned darts.

At home, I was powerless. But out here, I would become more powerful than he could possibly imagine.

9

My arm ached where something small and hard had been pressing into it.

I'd fallen asleep, my head tucked into a pile of leaves and my backpack clutched in my arms. The lights were all off in the DAR house now except for the streetlamps overhead. My stomach cried out for food.

Capitol Hill transformed at night. People were everywhere, streaming into restaurants and cafés, used bookstores and clubs, as dark figures lurked in doorways. I had to keep moving.

By now, everyone would know I was gone—first my family, then my friends. Then Asher.

As long as they believed it was a kidnapping, everything

could stay as it was—except without me. My parents could continue to look the other way, and Dad could keep his job. Asher wouldn't destroy my family as easily as he dismantled me.

I pulled my hood closer around my neck. My street power might make me invisible to the general populace, but I had much to learn about hiding from people like Stench. Even the memory of his odor pricked my nose.

I tucked my hands in my pockets and set off in search of a place to spend the night. After my encounter with Stench, finding the guitar boy was more urgent than ever.

The later it got, the easier it was to hide in shadows. It had to be eight or nine o'clock already—it got dark late in August. There were still grey and pink streaks in the sky.

All the good spots seemed to be taken—bushes, apartment bins, the alley behind the school. A lot of people seemed to be going in and out of the church, and the warm smell of something—chili, maybe?—wafted out of the open door. If I could sneak my way into that church, there had to be a million places to hide. But not tonight, when there were so many people going in and out. I would lose my invisibility the moment I crossed the wrong threshold.

Eventually, I ended up back on Broadway, lured by lights and the smell of Dick's Drive-In french fries.

The line was long, long enough that even Stench would probably stay away. A trio of kids leaned against the brick wall of the bank, and they looked familiar—a skinny girl, a short, wiry guy, and a taller one in the shadows. The girl sucked on a cigarette not much slimmer than she was. She looked like she could use some french fries, too.

I couldn't make out the tall boy's face, but something about him seemed even more familiar. Could he be the one I was looking for? He didn't have a guitar with him, so I couldn't be sure. And I wouldn't approach him with the other two standing by.

I got my fries and gulped them down, salty warm goodness filling me with courage. The boy's eyes were on me as I gobbled fry after fry. It couldn't be him—he looked angry, and every fry I ate seemed to darken his face more. Like Asher. It was time for me to go.

In the end, I found a place to squat—a garden shed of a carport at some house, full of plastic bags and big enough for a person to curl up. I could wait until the homeowners left for work in the morning, and come back after they'd gone to sleep for the night. It wasn't ideal, but at least I could hide from Stench until I found what I was looking for.

The next day went better—Stench disappeared, and I wondered if maybe he'd moved on. I stayed on the other side of the street from Mohawk, as I decided to call the hulking boy who'd tripped me, and the girl who hung on his arm. The two of them shared cigarettes while bullying change out of anyone who walked past. After awhile, the cops came and drove them off, and I found my way into the Starbucks.

It wasn't as easy to use the bathroom this time—Bach the

barista wasn't there, and the girl at the counter wouldn't give me the key until I bought something. So I invested a dollar twenty-five in an oatmeal cookie and a quick bath in the sink. A fresh coat of eyeliner made me look more like a student than a vagrant. Maybe today I could find a supply closet in the school or church and plan my future.

Police cruised through the neighborhood on a regular basis, but none of them seemed to be chasing me. What if I turned my cell phone on? Would there be a hundred text messages from Neeta and one curt voice mail from Asher asking me what the hell I thought I was doing?

I couldn't risk it. One weak moment, and they could GPS me within a mile. Then the police would be all over the neighborhood. Hopefully, they'd start by looking for a kidnapper. That would keep them from hauling kids off the streets.

As it was, I seemed to have come to a nonverbal agreement with the others—I stayed away from them, and they stayed away from me. After a few days, I started to get my bearings. I had food. I had shelter. I had purpose.

Then Mohawk showed up.

He towered over me, a good two heads taller and three bodies wider, like a human refrigerator. "You need protection."

"What do you mean?" I asked warily. If I needed protection from anyone, it was him. Him and Stench. Up close, he had a strange twitch to him, like something was crawling under his skin. He couldn't seem to keep his hands off himself.

"Maybe you're not really getting it yet. I saw that old junkie with you. He's been looking for you. He asked me about you. If you want, I could take care of you." He took a step closer and put his hand on my arm. "Of course, you'd have to do something for it."

I stepped backward. "Stay away from me." So that's why those girls were hanging out with him. What did he make them do to pay the price? Out of nowhere, a picture of me in Asher's apartment flashed through my mind. But that was different. Nothing could make me want to be with someone like Mohawk.

He stood rooted to the spot, scratching the back of his hand in a rhythmic motion. "If you think you're gonna survive out here without protection, you're gonna find out the hard way." I started walking fast, and his voice carried.

"He's gonna rape your ass, you stupid bitch! Then you'll be crying for me." I crossed the street and dove into the used bookstore, his words still ringing in my ears.

10

Now that I was on the street, I realized I had no plan and only a tenuous grasp of my street powers. If I had to buy something at Starbucks every day to use the bathroom, my money would run out fast—even faster in fall and winter, when I would need a coat, a pair of boots, a dry place to sleep. I would spainge, but I would not go crying to Mohawk no matter how desperate I got.

By then, maybe I would find the boy with the guitar. I recognized myself in his music. The memory of it gave me hope.

A few days passed without seeing Stench. Mohawk stayed on his side of the street, and I stayed on mine. How he could stay so huge when I was losing a pound a day, I didn't know.

Pretty soon I'd be as skinny as that mousey-haired girl with him.

No one talked to me except for one girl with a shaved head and haunted eyes, who said, "Hope it's worth it. This place will eat you alive from the inside out."

So would the life I left, I thought.

At least I was able to breathe. My inhaler supply would last for a while if I could stay away from triggers and remain calm, but I kept one in my pocket just in case. Eventually, I'd have to find some way to get more.

I found the police weren't looking to find me—they were looking to harass me, any chance they got. "Hey you," one shouted from his cruiser, "get outta here and go home or I'm gonna bust you, ho." The haunted girl's words came back to me.

Just when I thought I was safe, Stench reappeared.

I passed by the alley behind Neumos, which I'd learned served as a latrine for the street population. My hair, white and cropped, stood out, even on a sunny day. He spotted me in a heartbeat and grinned a black, jagged grin.

"Hey, sweetheart," he cooed. "I've been looking for you."

I bolted toward the Safeway—neither *safe* nor the *way,* because they thought I was one of the shoplifting crowd. Their red vests stood out like police uniforms, and their usually friendly faces turned dark the second I came through the door.

"Can I help you with something?" one of the Safe-bots

asked, then under his breath added, "Go to a shelter, why don't you."

I didn't have time for this. I headed toward the other door via the produce section. Safe-bot must have thought I was going to tuck apples under my shirt, because he followed me, and suddenly I felt like I was dragging a crazy, menacing train in my wake. I clutched my backpack and headed for the other door. I would make a run for it through the parking lot and somewhere . . . anywhere.

The doors whooshed open to a blast of sunshine and warm air. I looked behind me to see if the Safe-bot followed, and suddenly a bulk of canvas and sweat and fear gripped me in its arms. My scream muffled into his chest, suffocating me with fabric and stink.

"That's right," Stench whispered in my ear. "Come to Daddy." I fought, but his grip was too strong. He started to drag me along the wall to the back of the building.

"Hey! Take it somewhere else!" the Safe-bot shouted.

Stench twisted me so he could put his hand over my mouth. The smell of his skin overpowered me, hurling me into a state of panic and nausea. I had to calm down.

Safe-bot looked back and forth between me and Stench.

Stench chuckled, his hot breath on my ear. "Sorry about my daughter," he said as I wrestled to get myself free. "I hope she didn't steal anything." He tightened his hold, using my backpack to pin my arms.

The Safe-bot was about to go. I was invisible to him, a

throwaway human. I had no other options.

I bit the palm over my mouth as hard as I could, and Stench yanked it away. *STOMP HIS FOOT!* my brain screamed. I lifted up my heel and slammed it down hard.

He staggered backward, still holding my backpack in his hands.

I slipped out of the straps and ran—down the street and past the brownstones and the trees and St. Mark's Cathedral and into the Cornish College of the Arts parking lot, toward the heavy doors of the school.

Summer students were milling around the labyrinth of hallways. I didn't stop until I found the women's bathroom, where I counted my breaths to calm the hollow rattle I could feel rising. I pushed away the thought that Stench had taken all but one of my inhalers. For now, I only had to breathe.

I must have looked like a ghost, because when I ran in, a girl not much older than me with a baby carrier strapped to her chest caught my eye in the mirror. She spun around.

"Are you okay?" she asked. The baby, tucked against her and wearing a pink striped hat, watched me with huge brown eyes.

"Y-yeah," I said after a moment. The girl bounced a little, and the baby kicked her legs.

"You sure?"

I caught sight of myself in the mirror—ghostly, yes. My heart pounded with glee, shouting *alive, alive, alive.* I didn't have my backpack anymore, but I was still breathing. Maybe this was a test, to see if I was serious.

"Yeah. Thanks." I disappeared into one of the stalls. If I stayed here long enough, maybe I could figure out what to do next.

The cell phone in my pocket strained against my hip, grazing the secret mark of Asher's power.

I would not call.

I would not give up.

I would survive, no matter what.

11

Chop Suey looked completely different in the twilight as I made my way back to the garden shed—just a brick building with blacked-out windows and a signboard, not like a hopping club. A crow meandered back and forth on the sidewalk like a sentry—every time I saw one, it sent a shiver down my spine.

"We *have* to go to Chop Suey this Friday. Freezepop is playing," Neeta had said earlier this summer, when she'd invited me to hang out with her, Ellerie, and Ari. Asher was working at the crow lab that day, so I had no excuse to say no.

When Ari snorted and the rest of us looked at her dumbly, Neeta said, "You know . . . Rock Band? *'Frontload'*? It's an all-ages show."

"Yeah," drawled Ari, "that's exactly what I'm worried about."

"Shut up," Neeta glowered playfully. Since she'd been hanging out with Ellerie and Ari, Neeta's new passion was music games. Apparently Ellerie had Rock Band and every sequel, and they'd spent the last six months pounding out tunes. Ellerie was actually pretty decent on the drums, but Ari's less-than-enthusiastic guitar couldn't get them past the next batch of songs. Neeta had the pipes, and she wasn't afraid to use them.

Right now, she was belting out lyrics to "Frontload." *Got me feeling incredible . . . got control over meeeee . . .*

"I think it would be fun," Ellerie added, tapping her hands on the dashboard.

"Joy?" Neeta looked at me, her eyes pleading. "Asher could come, if he wanted."

If only she knew what powers were controlling me. "Yeah, sure. I'll ask him," I said slowly. I already knew what he would say.

But he surprised me by saying yes.

A few days later, in just a clingy dress and the bracelet, I huddled with the girls on the sidewalk outside Chop Suey. Each of us held foamy lattes from Stumptown Coffee—all except for Ari, who sipped an Italian soda from a straw poised suggestively between her pearly pink lips.

Asher would be here any minute. My friends were impressed by him—Asher Valen, obscenely wealthy View Ridge Prep boy with a passion for crows, who had somehow taken an interest in me. Ellerie and Ari pumped me for the details of our courtship as Neeta silently braided tiny braids in her hair. Had I met his dad? What was he *like*?

I had met his dad, but only on a few occasions involving hundreds of people at one event or another. He'd sniffed in my general direction—that is, until I warranted a closer inspection. When my dad was on the hiring block.

The Seattle IMAX was launching the world premiere of the latest 3-D sci-fi flick. The director was there, chatting with an exclusive group who had donated large sums to his wife's educational charity. He had a household name and everyone clamored to get close, even the shiny people with star status of their own. *That's the guy from Black Eyed Peas,* Asher whispered about one. *And that's the director's wife.* He pointed out a beautiful blonde. So it surprised me when the director approached Asher's dad as if Mr. Valen were the celebrity.

Later, Mr. Valen came to Asher's side and gave me the once-over. *So you're Joy Delamere,* he said. *I've been assessing your father.* His eyes were so sharp and grey just like his son's, and I felt the same chill I did when Asher was assessing me. Only when his father did it, it made me a little sick. I'd heard he got a girl kicked out of View Ridge Prep. I could only imagine what he could do to me.

"Yes, I've met his dad," I told Ellerie and Ari. "He seemed nice enough." Luckily he judged both me and my dad worthy, and I never had to be scrutinized by him again.

The subject shifted to Asher's attractiveness. "He *is* pretty hot," Ari observed, taking a loud slurp from her soda.

I warmed at the suggestion, because it was true. He melted me down and brought me back to life, poured into a new mold. That's how I knew he loved me.

So when Asher showed up at Chop Suey that night, his ratty Daft Punk T-shirt only added to the aura surrounding him already. Ari and Ellerie smiled shyly as he held me close.

Tonight's crowd was a mix of gamers, suburbanites, and kids with nowhere else to go. A mass was already building for the opening band, Ming & Ping, who were playing a feverish mix of Hong Kong electropop. A wall of all-ages sweat hit us as we entered.

Once we were in the club, Ari headed straight for a trio of street kids. A tall boy with a guitar case slung over his shoulder receded into the shadows, flanked by a shorter boy and a gaunt girl with spiky hair who looked like one puff of smoke might blow her away.

"What's Ari doing?" Neeta whispered to me.

"What do you *think* she's doing?" Asher exhaled, giving her a look familiar to me—the one where she's supposed to come to the conclusion that every word out of her mouth was equivalent to windshield spatter. When Neeta said nothing, he spelled it out patiently. "She's trying to score with the Ave Rats."

Neeta frowned. "Drugs?"

Ellerie wasn't paying any attention—she was too busy looking for band people in the crowd. Balloon Boy was here, a kid who showed up at every all-ages show with a bag full of balloons, which he twisted into shapes and tossed into the throng. I think his mom had dropped him off.

A few minutes later, Ari came back pouting. The Ave Rats, as the homeless underage population was known, traveled in packs, bound more tightly than family. I couldn't fathom the kind of loyalty that would share socks, share needles, share blood.

"Poor little rich girl didn't find what she was looking for?" Asher baited. He gave her that half smile he gave me, when he knew he was in control.

"The big one said, 'Sorry, I'm not the guy you're looking for.'" She imitated a deep, scornful voice.

The short boy with black hair looked over. He might have been cute if he cleaned up a little bit. The girl looked skinny but scrappy. I wouldn't want to mess with her. I couldn't make out the tall one's features, but I knew he was watching.

"What was that all about?" Neeta demanded. "Were you trying to buy drugs?"

I shrank a little in embarrassment. Ari rolled her eyes. "I just wanted to see if I *could*, Neeta." She slurped her soda. "Apparently he's *not that kind of boy*."

Asher tilted his head and eyed her appreciatively. "Ah, so now the truth comes out."

Ari tilted her chin. "You don't know anything about my truth, Crow Boy," she challenged. I couldn't fathom talking to him that way. "He's pretty steamy, though," she said slyly.

"Maybe he's *another* kind of boy. I mean, he could totally be her pimp. Do you know the kind of stuff that goes on around here?"

Ellerie came back from scoping out the crowd. "What kind of stuff?"

Ari gave her a knowing look. "We're talking about homeless teen pimps."

Ellerie's eyes went wide. "Did you see one?"

"Shhhh," Neeta hissed. Ellerie craned her neck to get a better view of the alleged pimp.

Ari giggled flirtatiously and poked Asher. "There are four of us and one of you, Crow Boy. You could be *our* pimp."

The short boy looked over his shoulder again, and skinny Ave girl scowled in our direction. The tall one in the shadows leaned closer to the other two like he was watching over them. A red light flickered on his face, and his eyes locked with mine.

In that moment I knew without a shadow of doubt that he was no pimp. There was something so close and knowing in that look. Vulnerable. No pimp could be like that.

"I mean, seriously," Ari was saying. "Can you imagine someone having that kind of control over your life?"

The tall boy stepped into the light, his gaze still fixed on us. On me. As if he were listening to my thoughts. A shiver passed through me, like he was taking an inventory and didn't like what he saw. I held Asher closer.

"Asher would make a good pimp," I said, almost to myself.

Ellerie chuckled, then stopped short. Ari put her hand over her mouth.

My heart began to pound in my chest. I tried to smile. "I mean, you could handle four women," I said lightly. "Not that I'd want you to."

I thought of how an unlit match could burst into flame from just a thread of smoke. A thread of smoke was all it would take to suffocate me.

I didn't want to look at Asher's face to see his reaction. He would explode, and then it would be over. Everyone felt it.

"C'mon, you guys," said Neeta, breaking the tension. "Let's dance. Look—the band is setting up—"

"So is Balloon Boy," Ari snorted. Ellerie giggled.

Seconds later, a cute East Indian guy with glasses came out onstage, the crowd crushed into the center, and even Balloon Boy calmed down enough to hear him shout out, *"This. Is. Freezepop!"*

And two seconds later, a guy on a keytar, another on the sequencer, and a girl with a hot pink streak came out and started rocking. But I wasn't listening. I was waiting for the moment when Asher would blow.

The shorter Ave boy pushed his way to the front, and I looked back at the taller one. His dark hair hung around his eyes, but he was still watching my every move.

"Are you okay?" Neeta asked, and I shrugged. Asher wasn't touching me, but I could feel his heat prickling my skin.

"Yeah. Of course!" I shouted, a bit too loudly over the

music. Neeta watched me a second longer and then let Ellerie lead her into the throng.

The melody pumped up the crowd with its electronic happiness, and even Asher's body started to move to the driving beat. I breathed a sigh of relief. Maybe he wasn't upset after all.

A little while later, Asher said in a low voice, "I'm going out for a smoke." And even though the room spun with music and noise and dancing, his words triggered a response. He meant for me to follow.

As soon as we were out of the club, Asher lit up a cigarette. He knew it could prompt an asthma attack. But if it did, he'd be right there to take me to the emergency room.

I followed him around the corner to the alley behind the club. He took a last swig of the beer in his hand and then threw the bottle viciously against the wall. I could barely see the shards of glass, shattered into a thousand pieces, through the tears suddenly springing to my eyes.

"Asher, I'm sorry," I breathed.

In a split second he gained control of himself. "*Now* you're sorry," he said quietly. "You wait until I'm upset to be sorry when you should have thought about that before you said it. What the hell, Joy?"

"Asher, I didn't mean to make you angry—"

But he was done with my excuses. Instead, his voice was heading to that dangerous, low pitch I knew well. "Do you think your family's going to be happy when I tell them I can't take care of your pathetic ass anymore? Do you think you're going to be sorry when your dad gets fired and he can't get a job in this whole fucking *town*?"

Dread coiled around my lungs. I counted to three, slowly, to try to catch my breath. Eyes closed. Calm. *One breath, two breaths, three breaths.*

"You're not looking at me," Asher seethed. "How can we have a conversation when you're not looking at me?"

He came in close and took my jaw in his hands, so close I could taste the sugar and smoke on his breath. I almost wished he would hit me, because then I would have a reason to call for help.

Instead, he pinched a lock of my hair and let it fall through his fingers. Gently. So gently. "Slowly," he said, helping me breathe. He held me up until my lungs recovered.

"Don't ever do that again," he whispered, his voice cracking, as if the pain of my betrayal had broken him. He kissed me on the cheek, and I melted into his arms.

"Sorry," I murmured. "So sorry."

I almost crumpled when he released me and I was left on my own two feet. "I'm going to get the car now," he said. "Be here when I get back."

Of course I would be here. As soon as we got to his place, I would show him how sorry I was and how grateful I was for his forgiveness. I blinked back the tears that came readily now that he was gone and wildly tried to wipe them away.

A sound startled me, the hum of a melody I didn't know. When I spun around, the tall boy with the guitar was standing there in the shadow of a doorway. I could tell by the look in his eyes that he had witnessed everything.

"I saw how he treats you," the boy said.

Around the corner I could hear the roar of a DeLorean coming closer. I felt utterly broken, but I couldn't break from his gaze. Any second the car would be here.

"If you ever need help, you know where to find me."

12

After his victory at the Safeway, Stench paraded around the streets with my backpack and gloated over his prizes. He'd taken most of my money and supplies and could probably make a killing with my drugs, if he didn't decide to use them himself. I was down to one inhaler, and I had to make it last.

That meant I had to manage breathing on my own. Outside of Chop Suey with Asher was the first time I'd had to do that in a long time. Normally I had three inhalers with me, and everyone else had extras. An asthma attack out here could be fatal.

What doesn't destroy me makes me stronger, Asher would say. I was stronger now than I had ever been. Besides, my backpack was one of the last things connecting me with my former life. Without it, I felt weightless. In a way, Stench had set me free.

When Stench went AWOL for a few days, it gave me a little breathing room. I hoped he used my cash to catch a bus out of town or drink himself to death under a bridge—good riddance. But I still had to figure out what to do next. I needed money. I needed meds. I needed a more permanent place to sleep. The garden shed worked for now, but any day I could get caught. My time was quickly running out.

The homeless boy—I'd seen him twice now. Didn't that mean something?

Neeta would think so. *If you see someone more than once, you are meant to cross paths.* That's what she said about our friendship. She'd moved to Issaquah with her parents when we were eight years old. We saw each other two times in that stretch of woods between our neighborhoods and had been friends ever since.

She kept calling me after the Chop Suey incident, and I avoided every call. "Why did you leave without telling me?" she demanded in the earlier messages. And then, when I didn't answer, the tone shifted. "What's going on, Joy? Why don't you call me back?"

I wanted to tell her, but there was nothing she could do—nothing I could do, short of running away, and that would mean leaving my family to take the fall. He might follow through on the threat against my dad's job. And what else? I remembered the bottle he hurled at the wall, the thousands of glass slivers.

They were just words now, and I could handle those. *Besides,* I thought, *it was only some of the time.* Telling Neeta would only make things worse.

When she finally reached me a few weeks after Chop Suey, she didn't ask any of the questions I knew were crowding each other to be heard. Instead, she said, "Let's go on a trip. No Asher, no Ellerie, no Ari. Just you and me."

I hesitated. We'd barely spoken for the last year, didn't even know each other anymore. Being trapped in a car for hours could make a person say things they didn't want to say.

"Come on," she urged. "We could go somewhere, anywhere you want. Maybe up to Bellingham to see Jesse."

My breath stopped in my throat.

Neeta couldn't help, but maybe Jesse could.

That one desperate thought took me all the way to Western with her, two hours in the car. I'd left without telling Asher, so I knew he would be furious. It didn't matter, though, because Jesse could help me. And then all of the secrets I'd been keeping for the last year could come out. He was always the responsible one—he'd know what to do about Dad and Valen Ventures. He'd tell me what to do about Asher. Maybe he'd even let me come stay with him for a while.

But that's not what happened. When Neeta and I showed up at the old house he shared with a bunch of other students, he almost slammed the door in my face.

"What are you doing here?"

It was nearly dark, and Asher would be getting out of the lab right about now. He'd call me soon, calling for his *little bird*, and I wouldn't be there. There would be consequences, I knew.

Just seeing me on his doorstep was enough to set Jesse off. "I have school, I have a job, I have a life!" he shouted, as if Neeta wasn't even there. "Get a *life*, Joy. I'm not responsible for you anymore."

Neeta and I didn't say much on the way home, only the bare essentials. Did I want to stop at Dairy Queen or Taco Time? It didn't matter. I couldn't eat. But I could pretend to sleep.

"You're different, Joy," Neeta said softly.

When we were younger, we'd gather a group of girls and lift each other one by one with our fingertips, chanting, *light as a feather, free as a bird. Light as a feather, free as a bird.*

We'd actually convinced ourselves that we could fly, until the one time I'd had an asthma attack midflight and everyone dropped me in shock—all except Neeta, who was still holding my hand.

I was falling now, and she was reaching out. But it was already too late.

After dark, I headed back to my garden shed. Home, sweet home. As long as I arrived at night and left before dawn, I might be able to get a few more days out of it.

My Vans scraped along the sidewalk in a quieter part of Capitol Hill, and I tried not to think about what was happening at home. A flap of rubber came loose, reminding me I'd need better shoes soon. I stopped to tug at the rubber, and a rock skittered behind me.

Suddenly, I was on high alert.

An oddly bulky figure was following a block or so back, his face dark in the shadows.

I picked up the pace and considered alternate routes. Broadway was a few blocks away, and my garden shed seemed like it was ten. He matched me step for step.

I was almost to Twelfth. I could head off to the right and see if I really was being followed, then maybe I could double back. Mohawk would be all too willing to protect me. How could I have been so stupid, to think the guitar boy would?

The man behind me turned the corner at Twelfth, matching my speed. I couldn't make him out in the pool of darkness, but a whiff of him sent me back to the struggle outside Safeway. The smell ignited my adrenaline.

Stench.

My pounding heart would set off a chain reaction. I had to slow down. *One. Two. Three.*

The park was up ahead and off to the right—I could run through the field, past the fountain, and maybe make it back to Broadway. I didn't actually know where Mohawk went at night, but I did know he'd added another girl to his harem.

What he extracted for his protection, I could only guess . . . but it had to be as bad or worse than what Stench had in mind. I shuddered at the thought.

The park was slippery under my Vans, the dampness soaking first into the canvas and then into my feet. A streetlamp lit the grin on Stench's face. I slipped and fell forward, streaking my hands with grass and mud. I wasn't fast enough. His boots squished through the green at an easy pace. Even if I ran, he was almost close enough to tackle me. I smelled the sewage embedded in his skin and clothes and breath.

Then all at once, someone pounced out of the shadows and tackled Stench, punching him first in the gut and then in the face—a wiry form, lean and strong, with dark wavy hair falling around his face. Whoever it was, I didn't stop to find out. I picked myself up off the grass and ran toward Broadway. I was a block away before I stopped to look back at the brawl. Stench was crumpled in a heap on the grass, and the other one strode toward me, lamplight bouncing off his figure and illuminating his face.

I knew him.

The one who made a promise in the alley, whose music made promises of its own.

He was right here in front of me, and he had just saved my life.

13

"It's you."

My lungs were still burning from the encounter with Stench, but I couldn't hold the words back.

Up close, he was even taller than I remembered, his eyes more cloudy, his hair a little longer. It hung in chocolaty strands around his ocean-blue eyes, which were watching me carefully. He wore the same clothes as when I'd seen him outside Hot Topic—an army surplus jacket, grubby jeans and tee, saggy black combat boots. Everything about him seemed familiar, as if we already knew each other. We *did* know each other.

He'd offered his help.

He wishes he could cure the scars, he'd sung to the deepest layer of my being.

"Do I know you?"

There was the voice—not angry or condescending, but . . . puzzled. And out of breath, from saving my life.

Slowly I felt the clench of my airways relax, and he waited for me to answer. I was still staring at him, willing him to recognize me. Didn't he recognize me? How could he not remember?

"I . . . I'm sorry, I didn't mean . . . I mean, thanks. Thanks for helping me with Stench." My voice felt strange in my mouth, and I realized I hadn't used it for days.

"Stench?"

I felt myself blushing. "That's what I call him, anyway."

He laughed, though not harshly. "It's as good a name as any—he smelled like . . . so wait, I've seen you, but how do you know . . ." He stopped himself as if he'd hit a wall. His eyes narrowed, looking deeper, and I had the sensation of total exposure. "What's your name?"

The word stuck in my throat. Joy was wrong. It didn't fit. *Tristesse,* I thought, would be better. Sadness.

"Triste."

It seemed true enough. Already, I had left Joy behind, the second I said good-bye to her in the mirror. I couldn't be her again.

He gave me a dark stare, then nodded. Like he knew it was fake, but it would satisfy him for now.

"What about you?"

His face clouded over. Did he recognize me from Chop

Suey, and from the sidewalk outside Hot Topic? Could he see into me now the same way he could then?

"We've been watching you for days—you're new around here, aren't you?"

The clothes and the hair—they'd be enough to fool everyone from my old life, but not him.

"Yeah," I said carefully, "but—"

"Wait," he interrupted slowly. "*Wait*. I know who you are."

A bubble of hope rose in my chest. I knew it. "You remember me!" I cried. I was almost laughing as I said it, laughing with happiness and relief, that he could see through my pathetic disguise.

Until I realized he wasn't laughing. Far from it. His eyes had gone stormy, his hands clutching the hair away from his face so that the veins and sharpness of his forehead were thrown into high relief.

"No. Oh no," he was saying. "Oh no, you can't be. *Damn*."

I was stunned. I'd thought, once I met him . . . something was there. A spark. He had to feel it, too. So different from Asher, something I couldn't quite place.

He continued to stare at me in horror. "Did I meet you at Chop Suey?"

I nodded, not daring to look at him.

"Yes, and you were . . . you were outside, crying . . . no, you can't be here. What are you doing out here?"

"But you said—"

"I know what I said." He was pacing now. "No, I don't

know what I said. I didn't tell you to run away." The last part he muttered to himself. "Did I?"

The hunger and utter fatigue after being out here for days and days suddenly hit me like a flood, a vast wall of disappointment. I had a made a huge mistake. The enormity of it could easily crush me.

"Yes," I said, my voice trembling. "You said if I ever needed help, I should find you." I couldn't keep the hurt out of my voice. I slipped my hand in my pocket and felt the scars through the fabric, the ones I thought he could somehow see.

But that, I knew now, was completely delusional.

"Well, you should get out of here," he spat, his face darkening into the same anger I'd first seen at Chop Suey, when he watched me with my friends. With judgment, I was realizing now. Not at Asher and his cruelty, but at me.

"Go home," he continued. "This is no place for somebody like you."

It felt like a slap. But he'd made a promise, *dammit*. The tears, the damn tears, they were threatening to fall. The only thing that could stop them now was to get angry.

"What's that supposed to mean? Somebody like me?" He'd seen what Asher had done to me, first with words and then with fire. Hadn't he?

"If you knew . . ." He trailed off, pressing his lips together. "Look at yourself. You can't even find a place to sleep on your own. How long have you been out here? Are you eating garbage yet?"

I must have made a face, because his voice split with frustration. "Because that's what it takes to survive out here. You'd be better off going back home, before something even worse happens to you. Trust me."

Asher would laugh, if he could see me now—my inhalers gone, no food, nowhere to go, chased down by some scary homeless guy. Like a helpless, abandoned bird that had fallen out of its cage. I knew exactly what would happen if I turned back now.

"No," I said. "I'm not going home. And who are you to tell me to? What are you doing out here? Where do you sleep?"

He gave me a hard look, made harder by the set of his jaw.

"At least tell me where I can go," I said softly. "Someplace safe."

I couldn't tell what he was thinking, but his shoulders slumped. A stray drop of rain landed on his face, like a tear from the sky.

Abruptly he turned. "Come on."

"Huh?"

"Come on! Unless you want to spend another night in a shed waiting for that asshole to come back for you."

How did he know I'd been sleeping in the shed?

"Besides," he continued, "sooner or later, they'll see you and call the cops. You can come with me, or you might as well turn yourself in right now."

While we were talking, I didn't even realize Stench had gotten up and was now limping across the park with murder in his eyes. He would come back—there was no doubt in my mind. Then there was Mohawk, who couldn't wait to get his hands on me.

Could I trust him? I'd been so wrong before.

"First, I want to know your name."

He smiled, breaking through the roughness of his exterior and giving me a glimpse of the person I thought I knew. "It's Creed."

Creed. Like a code of honor. He held out his hand, rough and cracked with dirt.

I had no choice but to take it.

14

Creed walked fast, taking strides with his long legs. He was six foot three, maybe, plus the boots. Next to him, I felt the safest I had since leaving home, like none of the last few days were real. Only he was real.

"Where are we going?" I asked.

"You'll see. But pay attention. You'll need to be able to find your way back, if everyone decides you can stay."

"Everyone?" There were the two I'd seen him with, but were there others? What would I have to do to be able to stay?

We turned down streets no longer familiar, into the valley where Elna Mead High School straddled a continuum of richer and poorer neighborhoods east of downtown. Pretty soon we came to a dilapidated street. I never would have come here without Creed. Chain-link fences surrounded sagging houses with sheets across the windows. Huge dogs barked in yards.

"Stay away from those," Creed warned. "They'll give you away faster than anything else."

"It's not a bad idea, though—getting a dog," I said nervously. If I'd had one, it could have taken a big bite out of Stench, even if it would mean scrounging food for two.

Creed stopped in his tracks and stared down at all five foot four of me. "Oh, no. Not you, too." He started walking again and I scrambled to keep step.

"What?" I laughed. "What?"

He grunted. "One pet is enough."

"Someone has a pet? Who? A dog?"

Creed scowled and walked faster, past a dark park with a low chain fence. "*No*, not a dog. A *ferret*." He said it with total disgust, in exactly the same voice my dad used when Jesse wanted to get a pet boa: *There is no way I'm buying rodent dinner for anyone living in this house.*

"A dog would be useful, at least," he mumbled. "Instead, we're tracking down cat food for an overgrown rat which smells like . . ."

I giggled, and he gave me an exasperated look. The idea of it astounded me, that this boy who could see right through people would spend his time finding food for someone . . . something else. I couldn't see Asher doing that for anyone, ever.

"Yeah," I interrupted, "but it gets pretty cold at night, and it could be nice to have a warm, furry little guy to curl up with . . ."

He rolled his eyes. "You sound exactly like Santos."

"Santos? Is he the short guy?"

He gave me a look, and my throat stopped working. Too many times with Asher, I'd said the wrong thing. Here was my chance to start over.

"Don't ever say that to him." When he smiled, I relaxed.

We turned another corner and Creed stopped, the most serious of looks on his face. "I don't know all of what brought you here, Triste, but you need to understand: You have to be tough on the street. You can't be weak. If you are, you'll never survive. You might want to think about that when you're weighing what's behind you with what's in front of you."

I wondered what had brought *him* to the streets, what frightening thing could bring someone so strong to his knees. Whatever it was, I couldn't imagine.

"Where is your guitar?" I asked.

Once again, he stopped, forcing me to bump into him. The smell of him, gritty and sweaty but still sexy as hell, filled me up and made me a little bit tipsy. He brought my hand up to his face to inspect it in the faint streetlight. My grey polish hadn't chipped off yet.

This was it, the moment I dreaded. He wouldn't understand why I had to disappear, why I couldn't just dump Asher and start over.

He would look into my soul, and he would hate what he saw.

"You know about my music," he said quietly. His gaze softened. I saw recognition there—not of my face, but of something deeper. Warmth spread from my hand to my heart. "How did you know?"

A smile played on my lips. Two could be mysterious. "Let's just say, I've been watching you. And there are a few things I've noticed about you, too."

Creed led me down a short alley and held his finger to his lips. We crept up to a house, boarded up and marked with graffiti, staircase broken through and rotting. It looked like a haunted house, the way it loomed over us. I saw a rustling inside, so quick I wasn't sure if I'd seen it at all.

Creed crouched under the staircase and yanked a panel to reveal a hole barely big enough for one person. The house, probably a hundred years old, would have a basement. All of the old houses in Seattle did.

"Careful," he whispered. "I'll go in first and then catch you."

My adrenaline picked up as he sat on the ground and slid through the hole. "Come on!" I could only see the tips of his fingers, reaching up for me. "Don't worry, I've got you."

I sat on the edge, careful not to hit my head on the fallen stair boards. One good gash would land me in the hospital, and then they would find me for sure. His hands touched my thighs, and I slid . . . down into his arms. The light from the hole lit his face enough for me to see his eyes on my lips. My arms were around his neck, heart pounding so much I thought he could feel it, too.

He let me get my feet under me before releasing me onto the concrete floor. "You okay?" I nodded, not at all sure if I could speak coherently when his hands were on my hips.

A rickety staircase led to another floor. "It's safe, but better to walk on the left." The boards creaked under our feet until we reached a door, barely ajar and glowing with an eerie, flickering light.

"It's me," Creed called, and I heard someone's sigh of relief.

"Shit, man. You scared us." The short boy—Santos, apparently—was holding up a board with thick, twisted nails through it. He relaxed and let the board drop to the ground as I came in behind Creed. "You should have—wait a second. Who the hell is she?" He looked mad. "You picked up 'Burbs? What the hell are you thinking?"

'Burbs? I looked up at Creed, whose face was a mixture of embarrassment and annoyance. "Shut the hell up," he said. "She's with us, at least until she figures out what to do next."

We were in the middle of a tiny kitchen with peeling wallpaper—or at least it probably used to be a kitchen, before somebody ripped out most of the cabinets and appliances and left only a few wires. A chunky candle flickered on the counter. Santos stood in a doorway leading into what must have once been a dining room. But the thing that hit me was the smell—musty, moldy, ancient, and like somewhere in the house, a sewage line had burst.

"Pick up another stray, Creed?" a birdy female voice called from another room. "Fuck. Just when I was getting to like being the only girl around here. Where the hell is she going to sleep?"

Santos was looking more and more agitated. "Hey!" he yelled into the other room. "Shhh! Do you want us to get busted over *her*?"

Languid footsteps shuffled in. It was the girl with dark choppy hair, looking as gaunt as ever. Close up, I could see faint purple scars on her face and the tightness of skin around her enormous eyes. She looked like a walking skeleton.

She gave me the once-over, too. "Oh, it's you." She gave Creed a withering look. "I knew sooner or later, you'd break down. You just have to protect everybody, don't you? Well, as long as there's enough room for the rest of us, you can keep her."

"Keep me? What does *that* mean?"

Creed once again was wearing a mask of annoyance. Apparently it was hard to keep his posse under control.

Santos shook his head and rolled his eyes at the moldy ceiling. "Ignore her. Hear that, May? I told her to ignore you."

"Whatever," she replied.

I wasn't quite sure, but I thought I saw Santos smile. Something moved inside the chest of his hoodie and a tiny striped face popped out—the infamous ferret. It crawled up onto his shoulder in one fluid movement and wrinkled its nose at me, as if I were the stinky one. Santos pushed it back down.

"Hey," he said to me, "you need the grand tour." Santos' eyes flickered toward Creed. "Then I gotta go."

"Wait a second," the girl, May, called from the next room. "What's her name?"

Santos looked at me expectantly.

"Triste," I said slowly.

"Triste," Santos shouted over his shoulder.

"Shhh, keep it down," hissed Creed.

"Yeah, right," May drawled in her high, thin voice. "Well, I like 'Burbs better."

Santos laughed. Creed closed his eyes, like he couldn't believe this was happening. "Go," he said to Santos. "Just go."

"I could give her the tour," May called.

"No!" Creed all but slammed his hand on the cracked counter. "I'm going to give her the tour."

"Okay, but you know how much I'd love to show her the shit room," May said. Santos snorted.

Creed held open the door to the basement for Santos. "Be careful," he said, and Santos gave me a two-finger salute before darting down the stairs. "Don't wait up for me," he called, and then disappeared into the darkness. Creed closed the door behind him, took a candle from a drawer, and lit it.

Another doorway led toward the front of the house. The entry glass had long ago been broken out, with only a few pieces still wedged in the doorframe. Everything was boarded up, with just a scatter of light from the outside.

Around the corner a wooden staircase led to the second floor. Trash and wood and plaster exploded everywhere, as if whoever used to live here sledgehammered the place up before leaving it for good. I realized the horrible smell was coming from a closed door under the stairs.

"That would be the . . . ?" I trailed off, pointing toward the door.

Creed looked embarrassed. "Uh, yeah. My advice: take a candle and hold your breath. This house is ancient—no running water for a while now, but at least it's a roof. You'll be glad when it's winter, if we don't get kicked out before then."

When it's winter. So he had already factored me that far into the future. The thought of it tore me in two between scared and pleased. With Asher, I never knew what the future held, or when his patience with me would finally run out.

"Watch out," Creed said as he led me up the wide staircase—sturdy enough to hold both of us, but not enough to keep the smell below from seeping up. Again, Creed looked embarrassed. "It's not as bad up there."

Upstairs, the smells of mildew and dust pressed into my airways. I would have to find more meds soon. My inhaler wouldn't last long in this environment.

There were three bedrooms—a big one with a mattress and two smaller rooms, with heaps of blankets and the same kind of trash littered downstairs. He led me to the larger room, where the battered guitar case was laid across the mattress. Most of the windows were boarded up. "We have to be careful about the light," Creed explained.

The glow from the candle softened his face. "Hey, I'm sorry about those two. They're a little jaded, but you can trust them."

He took me back down the stairs and showed me the long room on the main floor, ending with a stained, broken-down couch and May—doing the last thing I expected from her.

"What?" she demanded. "I like *Little Women*. Like you've never seen a person reading a book in your life, 'Burbs."

"May!"

She huffed. "Fine. *Triste*. What kind of pretentious fake name is that?"

"No worse than *May*," I shot back, a little surprised at my own boldness.

"Hmmph." And she went back to reading by candlelight. A library sticker wrapped around the spine of the book.

"What kind of person steals from the library?" I asked.

"*FYI*: I am a card-carrying member of the Seattle Public Library," she replied.

Creed sighed. "If you two think you can get along, we could go get some food." My stomach growled in response. It had been a few days since Stench stole my backpack. All I had left was six dollars—and the cell phone, waiting for me to turn it on and call home.

"Now there's something I can agree with," May said, sliding a flyer—one of those HAVE YOU SEEN THIS MISSING PERSON? ones—between the thick pages.

She caught me looking at it. "Don't even bother," she drawled, snapping the book closed. "We've all looked for ourselves on the missing persons flyers—the truth is, nobody gives a shit."

The three of us headed out into the darkness, quiet as mice until we'd scurried five or six blocks away. Creed walked with May on one side and me on the other.

"What should we have tonight?" Creed was asking. "Pizza?"

"God, Creed, you *always* want pizza. Don't you ever eat anything that doesn't involve bread?" Creed grinned, and I felt a pang. I wanted to know him well enough to know what he ate. I wanted to know all of them, even May, if she would let me.

We headed down the hill toward Madison. "How about Café Flora?"

Café Flora, I knew, was an upscale vegetarian place. "You have money?"

They both looked at me like I'd sprouted a fish head.

"Oh. My." May gave Creed the eye. "Where did you say you came from?" She looked at him in amazement. "You know, if you'd left her for a few more days, she might have starved to death and saved your hero instincts some trouble."

"May, shut up. Don't give her any crap."

"*Crap*? Oh, I see. New girl shows up and suddenly you have the squeaky-clean vocabulary."

"Hey. We didn't give you any when you showed up."

"That's because I didn't come from fucking *Bellevue*," she muttered. But then she left it alone. "So where *did* you come from?"

Fucking Issaquah, I thought . . . maybe even worse. "I—"

Creed cut me off. "I said leave it alone, May. She'll tell us when she's ready."

Whenever that might be.

We quieted down as we reached Café Flora, when May announced, "Okay, then. So apparently this is Ave Rat 101. Creed and I are going to teach you the finer points of Dumpster diving. Got it?"

"Uh, yeah," I said.

"Don't worry, it won't ruin your diet—though to be honest, if I was as fat as you, I would've killed myself already."

She did not just say that, Neeta said in my head. I was already on the lower end of the BMI and pretty sure I'd dropped a few pounds since I left home.

"Just ignore her," Creed said, opening the first Dumpster and bringing out a plastic garbage bag while I looked on incredulously. "It's not that bad," he said. "Trust me. Café Flora's got pretty good trash."

"Yeah, baby!" May called from inside the second Dumpster. "Jackpot! They've got pumpkin-stuffed tortellini again!

Seriously," she said, handing me a giant Ziploc bag of completely untouched pasta with sauce. "You've gotta try this stuff. But not too much—a moment on the lips, a lifetime on the hips!" She winked at Creed and even he couldn't hold back a smile.

15

May curled up on a pile of blankets in one of the smaller bedrooms while Creed and I sat on the mattress and talked—for hours, about everything from our favorite books to dreams to his music. Everything in the present—not the future, not the past, nothing about where we'd come from. Even though Creed knew about Asher, I didn't want to talk about him, let him control even this. I kept the crow bracelet high up under the sleeve of my flannel.

"So, how did you know I was new on the streets?" I asked. "Was I that obvious?"

Creed tilted his head back in a silent laugh. "You could say that."

"Hey," I said, "I thought I was doing pretty well." If my

own friends walked past, they wouldn't even see me. "Was it my clothes? My hair? Come on. What gave it away?" And would the police and Asher be able to see through my façade as easily as Creed?

He shrugged. "I don't know. It's a whole bunch of things. Clothes, hair, yeah, but more like how you carry yourself. You stand up too straight." I sat up, conscious of how I had slid down the wall next to him.

"So, it's my posture? You're telling me if I hunched a little more, I would fit in, no problem?"

"Okay, okay, it's more. I mean—well, you get to know who's out there, and it's pretty easy to spot the new people. But obviously you're not a foster case, and you have *no* idea what you're doing—"

"I managed to get this far, didn't I?"

"Yeah, and you just about got yourself dragged down an alley and murdered. You're lucky Maul didn't get a hold of you—"

"Maul?"

"Yeah. The big kid always out there, pimping his girls. That's his street name—he thinks he's all Star Wars badass . . ."

"Oh, you mean *Mohawk*. That's what I've been calling him."

Creed was suddenly on high alert. "What happened?" His body wound up, like he was ready to pound down someone's door and punch him in the face. If he only knew the ways Asher had already scarred me.

★ ★ ★

"But everyone already knows," I said to Asher, the night we reached the edge.

I knew punishment was coming but never imagined it could be worse than his words.

"I'm wearing the bracelet," I pleaded. "I never took it off once while I was away."

But I could take it off, and that was the point.

Asher drew back the sheets and laid me into the bed with great care, even if his voice sounded like molten steel. He wouldn't get my dad fired, or throw my family to the streets. I would do something else for him, something that would make it all go away. Then I would be forgiven.

Something flashed in his hand—his Zippo lighter. I remember thinking it was strange, because he never smoked in bed. It would be too risky, and he wasn't into risks.

But that wasn't what he was thinking. Instead, he lit a candle and then I saw something else glint in his hand.

"I don't care if anyone else knows," he said softly. "I only care if you know, Joy. You belong to me."

Creed was watching me like he was expecting an answer, and I realized his question was hanging in the air. What happened? Had Maul done something to me?

"Nothing, nothing," I said, taking a breath. "Mohawk . . . *Maul* . . . never did anything to me." But I knew I didn't sound very convincing.

"How do you know him? Did he . . . hurt you?" Creed scooted toward me on the mattress and tucked his arm around me—so close that if I turned my head, our lips could touch.

"No," I said, slowly, so he couldn't hear the tremble in my voice. "He didn't do anything but offer to protect me." There was a world of difference between being here with Creed and what Maul offered. "I said no thanks."

Creed glanced through the open door toward where May was sleeping. "He's no good, trust me. Stay away from him, okay?"

Had Maul done something to May? Creed's face defied a simple reading.

"So, tell me about street names," I said, hoping to shift him out of the treacherous sea of his thoughts. "Creed isn't your real name?" Any more than Triste was mine—but he didn't have to know that yet.

"Out here, your name represents who you are, and the more vulnerable you are, the tougher you want your name to be. Creed is who I am. If I used to have another name, it doesn't matter. I'm not that person anymore."

Every question he answered left me with a new one. Where had he come from? Who had he been before he became Creed? I wasn't Joy anymore, I knew. But would my new name show me who I was now?

"What about Santos?" From my limited knowledge of Spanish, I knew it meant both "saint" and "damned."

"He has that name for a reason."

I lowered my voice, even though I was pretty sure I could hear soft breathing coming from the other bedroom. "And May?" I couldn't fathom what her name was meant to identify. "Is that a fake name, too?"

"That's her real name," Creed said through a yawn, burrowing closer to me in the chill of the night. "She doesn't have anything to hide."

Santos came in long after the rest of us were asleep and the first streaks of grey were making their way across the sky.

"Hey," he said, making me jump.

I was still asleep next to Creed. Santos looked tired, like a very old spirit trapped in a boy's body. I didn't know where he'd been, and I didn't want to ask. "May in there?" He gestured toward the other room.

Creed nodded sleepily. Santos slipped in and curled up with her in the early morning light, the two of them like a couple of abandoned puppies.

"Are they . . . ?"

"No," Creed said, like it was strangest thing he'd ever heard. "They're family."

"Wait . . . brother and sister? But . . . how is that . . . possible?" May and Santos looked nothing alike.

"We're all family—the only family we've got. It doesn't have to be blood."

"But I don't understand . . . don't you have real family?" I winced, even as I said it, thinking about my own. A flash moved across his face, then it was gone, and a familiar feeling crept into my stomach. *Wrong, wrong, wrong.*

I wanted to say something funny to break the tension. But Creed was serious. Deadly serious.

"You don't have to tell me," I whispered, willing my tone to convey what words couldn't. I would give anything to know how Creed came to be.

He didn't speak. Instead, he slid closer to me and pulled me into his arms. I was too tired to stay awake, too aware of his arms around me and skin against mine and the rhythm of his breathing to even think about falling asleep.

16

When I woke up, I was alone on the mattress with a sliver of sunlight coming into the room. I had no idea what time it was, only that my stomach thought it should be lunch and my head thought I should roll over and go back to sleep. It felt incredible to wake up on something flat and soft, even if springs were poking through several unidentifiable brownish spots. The guitar was gone, too.

In daylight, it was clear that the house had been condemned for a reason. There was plaster torn away in jagged holes, wooden slats rotting away in a gaping mass. Swirls of dust followed an invisible current around the house . . . an asthma attack waiting to happen.

Santos was still curled up on the heap of blankets as I crept past, keeping my breathing slow and easy.

From downstairs came the welcome odor of coffee. *Coffee?* I no longer questioned the wonders and comforts my new friends were able to conjure. I only hoped they saved some for me.

May and Creed were sprawled on the couch sipping from Starbucks to-go cups, her legs dangling across his lap. *Like one big happy family.* They turned to me as I gave the room under the stairs as wide a berth as possible. May giggled.

"Want some? Sorry to say it won't be one of your Macchiato Skinny Latte Almond Split-Shots, and you might accidentally swallow some grounds, but it's not half-bad free coffee, if I do say so myself." She picked up a steaming cup from the floor next to her and held it out to me.

I popped off the top to inspect the contents—brownish water with a few floating bits and a swirl of cream—and took a cautious sip. Hot, bitter, with a hint of grit.

"Not bad," I said.

"Not bad? That's some quality brew, 'Burbs."

Joy, I nearly blurted out. "How did you get it?"

"Secrets of the trade," May answered languidly, stretching her toes out against Creed's stomach.

He snorted. "Used coffee grounds—any café has bags and bags of it they just give away. Then you get a cup—"

"That reminds me," interjected May, "don't wreck the cup—that's *your* cup now."

"— and the hot water and cream are free," Creed finished.

May opened up a waxy brown bag and took out a chunk of what looked like blueberry scone. "Want one?" She tossed me a brown bag of my own, and I opened it to find a bran muffin.

"Sorry," she said, "that's always the one they have left. Always bran muffins. Like we need any more shit around here . . ."

Creed tilted his head and glared, which, I realized more and more, was part of their routine. Part of becoming a family was finding your place in it. And despite the terrible air, I hoped there would be room to breathe in this one.

Suddenly, with a wild spiral of legs, May was off the couch and in my face. I'd thought we were about the same height, but now I realized I towered over her by a good three or four inches. How she made herself seem taller was one of the deep mysteries of May. "That reminds me," she mumbled with a mouthful of scone, "we've got to do something about your hair."

I tried to tuck it behind my ear, like I would have when it was long, but the ragged ends slipped through my fingers.

"Oh, no," said Creed. He got up from the sagging couch, a tweedy brown in the dappled light. "I'm outta here, before this gets ugly." He picked up his guitar. "May, you'll take care of her today?" It was more of a statement than a question.

"Hmmph," May grunted. She scrutinized me, picking up locks of hair and letting them fall limply. Other than the occasional quick scrub in a public bathroom, I hadn't bathed since I'd left. Two weeks ago? I'd lost track.

Finally she sighed testily. "Could you . . . sit down or something, so I can get a better look at you?"

"Um, okay," I said, feeling like the matter had already been settled long before I came on scene.

Creed disappeared around the corner. "I'll be back later," he shouted, then pounded down the stairs with his guitar.

I sat up straight on the couch as May ran her fingers through my scalp, still tender from my Manic bleach job.

"Oh my God. No wonder. Did you do this yourself?"

I nodded.

"Oh. Ouch. You totally burned your scalp." She combed through my hair with surprising tenderness. "Well, there's nothing I can do about the color until it heals, but at least I can give you a decent haircut. Don't tell me—you did that yourself, too."

I nodded again.

"Well, whatever it was you ran from, it had to be bad if you were gonna give yourself the fucking worst haircut I've ever seen. Wait here." A second later, she appeared with a pair of shears.

"Don't tell the boys I have these, or they'll use them to pull nails out of their boots or some stupid shit like that." She brandished the scissors in front of my face to emphasize the point.

"No problem," I said.

"Good. Well, I keep them hidden anyway. Those guys can do the most stupid-ass things and have no idea what they're wrecking. Now sit on the edge so I can reach you."

I sat obediently and she ran her fingers through my hair again. Bleaching my hair had turned my strands from thick and dark to white and airy, like cotton candy, more and more tangled each day. She finger-combed the strands until it felt like a rhythm.

When we were younger, Neeta and I used to do each other's hair—she would put dozens of braids in mine, and I would make ringlets of hers. My mom let us have slumber parties whenever we wanted—I think she felt bad I was so isolated. They never let me stay at someone else's house, just in case I came down with pneumonia or had a sudden asthma attack. Neeta was like a substitute sister.

May lifted my chin and arranged the strands one way and then another. "What are you doing?" I asked.

"I'm trying to figure out what's going to look the best on you. I mean, you've got these chubby cheeks." I frowned. "But then you've got this great sharp line to your jaw and big eyes, like Natalie What's-her-name—"

"Portman?"

"Yeah, whatever—but with white hair. So actually, if we gave you the right shape, you could totally work the grandma hair thing—"

"Grandma?"

"Do you want me to fix it or what? No. Don't answer. It couldn't get worse, so you might as well let me make it better."

Seconds later, I felt the shears tearing through the hair I had left, and little by little, it fell on the floor in fluffy white tufts. May paused to take it all in, then dragged the blades through more and more of my hair until we both heard the floor creak behind us. Santos rubbed his eyes with his fists, reminding me of my younger brother, Jonah. "Got any coffee?" he mumbled, staggering further into the room. His hoodie and T-shirt were rumpled and faded, pants hanging down around his hips.

"It's cold by now." May handed him the fourth cup where an "S" had been scratched into the waxy surface. "There's bran muffins in the kitchen."

"Wow, nice hair. She's Sid and Nancy now."

May rolled her eyes. "You can't be Sid *and* Nancy. But she doesn't look half bad. Here—take a look at yourself." She held up a shard of mirror. "We can fix the makeup later, but look at the cut and tell me what you think."

The blonde in the mirror blinked back at me—hair razored and wispy around the face just below the jaw, unlike the jagged chunks I'd left by grabbing the entire mass and hacking it off. It looked chic and punk, mean and sassy at the same time, making my round cheeks disappear and my chin look sharper. Suddenly, I looked like a badass. *Cross me if you dare.*

"Wow. It's the best haircut I've ever had," I said, and I meant it. May clearly had the street power of disguise.

"Whatever," she snorted. "But it's better than that post–Gene Juarez Salon look you had going on. Nobody is going to call you 'Burbs now." She giggled. "Except maybe us, because you'll always be 'Burbs to me. But you look hot now."

"Smokin'," Santos agreed, chomping on his muffin. He slugged half the coffee and then fed some muffin to the ferret, who sniffed around before swallowing a fingertip-sized bite whole.

"At least nobody is going to try to jump your ass," May was saying. "A few more weeks, and you'll actually look like you belong here."

Maybe I would look like I belonged. But the real question went deeper—I'd left one family and only accidentally found another. Would there be room in this one for me?

17

"Okay, so the first thing you need to learn if you're going to survive on the streets is how to shop."

Santos and I were down on MLK Way outside the Red Apple Market, where he seemed a lot more comfortable than me. As far as I could see, I was the only white person for about a mile radius, and if looks could talk, none of them thought my Sid-and-Nancy hair was half as cool as May and I had this morning.

On the way, he'd told me all about his ferret, Faulkner, "Named after my favorite writer."

"*William* Faulkner? You've read William Faulkner?"

"Course," he replied, like I'd suggested he couldn't read instead of reading one of the hardest authors assigned in my

English class last year. "You read him?"

"Yes . . . but I didn't think . . ."

Santos shrugged. "Course I read—everybody goes to the library. I liked *The Sound and the Fury* best—all those secrets, and how things in the past affect people, and how the same stories sound different, depending on who you talk to. And the one character who seems to be the weakest is the one who *knows everything*."

Now that we were in front of the Red Apple Market, Santos barked at me, "You're not paying attention."

My thrift-store PVC pants were too hot on a sunny day, but at least I'd left the flannel at the house. Asher's smell had almost faded by now.

"That's the first thing you need to learn, Triste—pay attention. Because if they think you're there to take stuff, they're going to pay attention to you." He crouched with his hands out, looking like a panther about to pounce. "You have to be quick. *Stealthy*. Not let them know what you're up to."

"But it's stealing," I protested.

"It's surviving," he retorted. "It's like that guy—the one who stole the bread and who got stuck in jail for a hundred years . . . Gene Val-gene—"

"Jean Valjean? From *Les Misérables*?"

"Yeah. Him. Anyway, who knows if you and me taking bread is going to lead to us being mayor someday, and if that would lead to a *whole revolution*—the homeless, the foster system, predators, adoption . . ." His eyes glowed. "*Everything* could change because of the bread you and I are about to take."

I thought of being in mock trials with Neeta—the two of us an unstoppable team. Neeta was the strategist. I formulated the counterargument. Then Neeta went in for the kill. But I couldn't think of a single counterargument to shoot down Santos's grand master plan for the food I was about to help him steal.

And suddenly I knew his street power with startling clarity: He could talk his way through anything.

"So here's the plan. You go in and scope out the bread aisle—actually, I'm kind of hungry for some Cheetos, too, so if you can, cruise through the chip aisle, okay? I'll come in after you and stay in the produce section. If you see somebody, you give me the signal—like," he glanced down at my Vans, "screech your shoe on the floor, and I'll know to lay low. But if the coast is all clear, pop your gum."

"But I don't have any—"

"Here," he said, taking the piece he'd been chewing out of his mouth and offering the greyish purple lump to me.

Ugh. "Don't you have any more?"

"Sorry, last piece." He shrugged. "But it's still got some flavor left! Grape Rage! Come on. Are you in?"

I hesitated.

"We'll get a new pack, I promise. All the gum is over on the magazine aisle, across from the ice cream."

"Mmm," I said involuntarily.

"You like ice cream?" Santos grinned at discovering one of

my deep and abiding weaknesses. "Okay, we can get some of that, too. Cherry Chip? Caramel Pecan?"

"Mmmm . . ." He was winning me over. "Wait a second. We're running out of room. What about Faulkner?"

"You're right! Here. You take him." In one continuous movement, he scooped the creature out of his hoodie and dangled him in front of me. Faulkner's pink paws stretched out in the air to discover what, exactly, had happened.

I took him, still warm from Santos' hoodie, and tucked him inside mine. Faulkner's sharp, musky smell clouded my nose as he laid his head on top of my breast.

Santos grinned. "See? He'll be fine. Now, back to the plan. . . ."

Fifteen minutes later, we really were Sid and Nancy on a wild ride in the grocery store—punks with a purpose. I had my Van-screech down and my signals straight. It wasn't just about bread and bubble gum—it was about freedom and our futures and the risks we would have to take to *be the change* we wanted to see in the world.

Santos cruised through produce while I staked out the bread aisle. He would be pocketing peanuts and a few apples, plus snacks for Faulkner, who had a weakness for cucumbers. Meanwhile, Faulkner tucked his tickly pink feet on my ribs and off-gassed a smell only a mother ferret could love. I held my breath and picked up the pace. Exactly like Santos said, there was a mirror above the meat and dairy cases at the back—offices behind one-way glass and cameras potentially everywhere. I hoped my haircut would hide my face enough not to appear on KING 5 news, the camera shot spliced next to my junior-class picture and the reporters declaring it "a definitive match." No loaf of bread was worth this—I would rather Dumpster dive after dark.

Santos rumbled his throat. All clear on the produce aisle, awaiting my signal to move.

Just then, a meat man came around the corner, as tall as Creed but a lot . . . meatier. He wore a white apron with smears of pink and glared in my general direction, like he was about to take me to the back and show me his collection of butcher knives.

My Vans squeaked on the floor. Oh, no! Was that the signal to move or stay put? Santos was going to kill me, I was so bad at this. So much for being the change. I practically tripped into the butcher's arms.

"Excuse me." I laughed like a crazy girl. "Is there a bathroom here?" I brushed my hair out of my eyes, letting the charm bracelet dangle. Maybe he would see it and realize I was just another normal.

He got a strange look on his face, sniffed the air.

Oh, no. He was smelling Faulkner. Or worse. Faulkner's fart.

He put his hand over his nose, as if my very proximity was sucking the oxygen out of his lungs. "Yeah, through those doors." He waved me away and kept walking toward the front of the store. "And *hurry*."

I pushed my way through the double doors to the warehouse in the back, deserted except for me and my new hero, Faulkner. Straight in front of me was a case of Cheetos—jackpot! I grabbed two bags and tucked them in around Faulkner, whose feet scrabbled against the plastic like it was his new playground. "Stop it," I hissed. While I was here, I might as well grab the half roll of toilet paper sitting on the back of the tank. God knew we needed some.

I peeked through the twin windows into the store. Santos would be an aisle away, wondering what happened.

On the desk was a pack of gum—open, and cinnamon, but it was better than nothing. I tucked it into my pocket and dashed through the door, hoping no one would notice the extra poof I'd gained in the last few minutes.

Santos was in the bread and cereal aisle, giving me the what-the-hell look. "Change of plans," I muttered as I shielded him from the one-way glass.

"'Bout time," he said. "I mean, I know the shit room is bad, but . . ."

"It was Faulkner!" I whispered, then imagined what this conversation would sound like one aisle over, and just like that, a giggle popped out, and then another, and then Santos started, and then it was pretty much impossible to stop. But we tried—because Meat Man came around the corner as Santos was stuffing the bread into his shirt and shouted, "Hey!" He wiped his sausagey hands on the apron.

Santos and I were trapped between Meat Man and the

back doors. I grabbed his arm and said, "Come on!" because I thought I remembered a door standing ajar where Meat Man must take his smoke breaks in between chopping things to little pieces, and if we ran *right now*, we could actually make it.

Santos followed me through the swinging double doors and there it was—a crack of light. If we were lucky, some other meat man wasn't out there, but we didn't have time to check. The first Meat Man was hot on our trail. But he wasn't fast like me or agile like Santos, who knocked over an open stack of Quaker Oats as we slipped out the door. We heard Meat Man swearing as we beat it all the way up the next block to the library bushes.

"You are one crazy chica, you know," Santos panted. "What the hell . . ."

I waited for the boom to drop—he would never take me with him again. I almost got us caught or maybe even killed by Meat Man. Asher flashed through my mind. I winced, shielding myself from whatever might come next.

Before I knew it, my throat was closing. I gasped for air and only felt particles creeping in, the dust from my clothes and Faulkner's fur and the terror of escape and now Santos's disappointment. Slowing my breaths was not enough.

I was going to suffocate.

In a flash, I whipped out my inhaler—it wasn't my emergency one, but it would have to be good enough.

"Hey," Santos said, his voice soft as the rest of the world spun around us. "Hey, are you okay?" He was putting his arm around my shoulder, rubbing my back with his hand. "Triste? Triste, are you okay?"

It took me a minute to respond. "It was Faulkner," I said, barely a whimper. Then it all came out in a rush. "The meat guy was coming, and he farted—"

"The meat guy?"

My breath was returning to normal. "No, no! Faulkner . . ."

Santos started laughing.

". . . and I didn't know what to do, I told him I had to use the bathroom, and I was back there and was thinking you were by yourself, and I didn't want you to think I'd gone back on the plan—oh yeah, then I tripped . . ."

Santos's laughter died down. "So you're sick," he said seriously.

Damn, I thought. *I shouldn't have resorted to the inhaler.* "Not really," I lied. "I just have asthma sometimes."

Santos frowned like he didn't believe me and pointed to my inhaler. "You're gonna run out of that shit sooner or later, though."

Faulkner popped his head up through the top of my hoodie, making a crunching sound against the Cheetos bag. I was grateful for the distraction. "Oh wait, here," I said with a sniff, pulling out the bag. "These are for you." I took the gum out of my pocket. "And this, too."

Santos snatched the bag and the gum like I'd just given him a birthday present. "Shit, girl, you're the best!" And he tore it open right there and stuffed a handful into his mouth.

"Whatever drugs you need, I can get for you. You just tell me. Okay?"

He gave a Cheeto to Faulkner, who crunched nuclear orange dust all over my hoodie. But I didn't care. Because Santos didn't care.

Santos was going to help me.

I was in.

18

I gave Santos a list of the meds I might need for any and every asthma eventuality, and he showed up a few days later with a sack full of drugs: Fluticasone inhalers, albuterol inhalers for emergencies, prednisone oral steroids, amoxicillin and azithromycin in case of bronchitis or pneumonia . . . all of it labeled haphazardly and in varying quantities, as if they had all escaped from the medication graveyard.

"Don't tell anyone I got this for you," he whispered, shoving the plastic bag into my hands.

I perused the contents. "Oh my . . . this is unbelievable. How did you get these?"

He grinned as if I'd just given him a huge compliment. "You know I could tell you, but then I'd have to *keel* you," he quipped in a gangsta accent. "Besides, I can't have you dying when I'm supposed to be teaching you how to live."

From then on, Santos took it upon himself to show me how to survive on the streets. "It's like that *Mice and Men* book," he declared. "There's Lennie, the slow guy, and George, who kinda, you know, watches out for him, and Lennie's got, like, this thing for rabbits. So I have to watch out for you and make sure you don't get yourself killed."

"So . . . I'm Lennie in this scenario? You're the one with the rodent."

"Ferret, *not* rabbit." Faulkner poked his nose out at this sound of his species. "And you're missing the point," Santos continued.

"Which is . . . ?"

"I gotta watch out for you."

"Right," I said. "Then you're going to shoot me at the end?"

"I doubt you'll be the first one to die," he said quietly.

If I were as fat as you, I'd kill myself, May had said. There had to be so much more to her story. More to all of their stories, if what Santos said was true.

Santos recruited May and Creed in my reeducation whenever possible. Most days they fell into a rhythm, going their separate ways during the day, then coming back together at twilight. Except Santos, who disappeared most nights as soon as it was dark and didn't get home until maybe three or four in the morning.

May fixed my hair, bleaching the top layer a white-white

and giving the layer underneath a cool blue hue. Santos taught me to be quick and invisible. Creed watched over all of us.

Creed never explained to Santos and May where I'd come from, and they didn't seem to recognize me from the club. The agreement between us was unspoken: Creed felt responsible. It would be just between us. And when we curled up together on the dingy mattress, I thought about how he made me feel safe but not crushed. He sang himself—and now me—to sleep.

I could fall for someone like that.

My friends and every other kid in King County were back in school now, which meant the rhythm and flow of Capitol Hill shifted to a steady stream of students heading into Seattle U and the community college. At least it was easier to sneak onto the campuses for the essentials now—clean bathroom and a shower now and then. Even Creed was starting to notice my earthy aroma.

"Okay," Santos said one day when he was showing me the finer locations for acquiring the necessary goods: soap, styling wax (for him and May), socks, and candy. Creed brought home a new backpack for me after I told him about the one Stench stole, though I left out the part about the meds. The last thing I wanted was for my health to become an obsession for him, too.

"Okay, so at some point," Santos said, "you have to decide what you're going to do with your life."

"Whoa, whoa, wait a second. So I'm planning my future now?"

We were walking down Broadway toward the Walgreens for a licorice run—not the Twizzler kind, but the long, red ropes you could hardly find anymore. They were practically impossible to stuff into a backpack silently, but Santos had mastered the art and promised to teach me.

Santos grinned. "Well, we all do something. We can't just steal bread all the time—though you're getting better, I'll admit. For a while there, I was worried we'd get kicked out of every market on my list."

I beamed at the compliment. "But I thought you said it was a moral imperative, that stealing bread was the first step to changing the world?"

Santos talked with his hands when he wasn't petting Faulkner or feeding him bits of cat food, and this time he waved a finger at me. "Don't get me wrong. Bread is the first step. Having a job—that's the next step. Everybody contributes."

Creed didn't play his guitar at the squat because of the noise, but he came back every day with a fresh pile of change in the case.

"So . . . Creed plays music. What does May do?" She could do hair, clearly, but I didn't know any salons hiring street girls.

"She does a bunch of stuff," Santos said vaguely. "I think she's got art students at the college who pay her to . . . you know . . ."

"She's a *prostitute*?" I blurted out, then covered my mouth. Santos looked injured.

"No! She poses. Like for drawing or whatever. She's a model."

"Huh. That doesn't sound so bad."

"Yeah. Well, maybe she can hook you up, too. They probably need more than one cute girl to draw." I looked at him sharply—he was blushing furiously. "I mean, you know, you're both . . ."

"*Cute*," I finished. "Figure-drawing models have to be more than cute. It's not like porn, you know."

He started laughing wickedly and looked away.

"Somehow, this feels so incestuous," I teased, then stopped. Maybe I was being presumptuous, thinking I'd penetrated the family circle.

"*Hey, baby*," he said in a fake Spanglish accent to the police car rolling to a stop in front of us, "would you like to buy my *seester*?"

I hovered behind Santos. The cruiser's window rolled down at an eerie pace. He clutched a flyer in his hands with a girl's face photocopied onto it. Joy's face. And mine.

The cop did not look amused. He held up the flyer. "Have you seen this girl? She disappeared about a month ago." I looked down at my shoes.

"She a runaway?" Santos asked, wary. None of us were friends of the police, who regularly harassed kids on the street.

"Could be," the cop replied grudgingly. "You seen her?"

"Hey," he called to me, leaning forward to get a better look. "You seen this girl?"

I cupped my cheeks in my hands, like I was looking closely at the picture—but really I was trying to hide my face. That and the wild pounding of my heart.

I slowed my breathing. They had to be looking for a girl with asthma. An inhaler would give me away in an instant.

It was last year's school picture, taken not long after I met Asher. I'd probably lost ten pounds since then—five when Asher thought I should, and five more since I'd been out here on the street. She wasn't me anymore. Those cheeks were too round, still smiling and innocent. She looked like a baby.

She deserved whatever she got with Asher, and probably more.

"She looks like some *cabrona*," Santos observed. "Why you looking for her here?"

The cop shrugged. "You sure you haven't seen her?"

"Hell, no," Santos said, a little too loudly. A couple of normals on the opposite corner looked over to see what was going on. "C'mon, Triste." He looped his arm through mine. "Hey, we don't bother you, you don't bother us."

"Watch yourself, *Rat*." The cop spat out the window and moved on.

"Let's get out of here." Santos was still holding my arm as we walked faster and faster, away from the Walgreens. The cop didn't follow. He'd already cruised past the next group.

I could barely catch my breath. I had to be way more careful from now on.

We never did make the licorice run.

After dark, Santos disappeared without saying a word to any of us.

"Where is he going?" I asked Creed, after May had gone to bed and he and I cuddled close to keep the chill away. Being so near was both a blessing and a curse.

"He doesn't really talk about it," Creed murmured into my hair.

"But he looks worse every time he comes back. Aren't you worried?" The last few times, he'd come in grey and exhausted and looking like someone had punched him in the jaw, then slept until midafternoon.

Creed let out a frustrated sigh. "I can't control him any more than I can control you."

But he could—he just didn't know it. Every time he touched me, I felt my nerves waking up as if from a long sleep. The more we stayed here together, the worse it would get.

I shifted so our foreheads touched and our breathing mingled. Our eyes couldn't help but meet. Candlelight flickered on his skin, prickly and unshaved for days. Up close, his eyes were a network of blues and greens and topaz under a shock of dark brown lashes.

"You have more control than you think you do," I said. His lips were only inches away. He didn't blink, only stared at me, weighing something I couldn't fathom.

"No." A pause. The moment was broken. "I can't control even the things I want to." He rolled over and blew out the candle.

"'Just gotta let it go,'" he sang softly. He didn't pull me close again.

With Asher, it was always so clear. After I'd given myself to him, there was no going back. He liked that I was a virgin—one of the things he liked best about me. He could teach me whatever I needed to know, which was everything. Every day after school, he picked me up in his DeLorean and took me to his private apartment. He would work on research while I did my homework. Then, when I was finished, he would do things to me that I never knew were possible, stripping away layer after layer of what separated us until there was nothing left.

Even when he was angry, I always knew how to bring Asher back to that sweet place. He would forget my words and focus on my body.

What was stopping Creed?

19

Creed and I downed the coffee May made for us one morning as he thumbed through the paper she'd snatched on the way. I avoided looking at newspapers, as if by avoiding them I could ignore what was happening outside of my cozy new world.

"The worst thing that can happen," Santos once told me, "is losing your squat."

"Getting kicked out by the police?" The thought made me shudder.

"Or worse. Getting the shit kicked out of you by someone taking over—if that happens, you're fucked. You lose your house, you lose your stuff, and if you're really lucky, you only lose an eye."

I pondered this.

"No shit. I had this friend . . . anyway, he lost an eye, and it wasn't pretty. Bled all over the place . . ."

He laughed, but underneath, I could sense the threat—that all of this could evaporate and leave us scarred for life.

After our coffee, Creed and I cautiously climbed out of the squat together. It was getting colder at night, now that it was late September. A layer of frost surrounded the entrance. Even though I hadn't come in or out of the house by myself yet, I still looked around each time. I couldn't stand the thought of losing it. Losing *them*.

The leaves were starting to turn—even in this sparse neighborhood of chain-link fences and ratty, weed-infested lawns. Higher up the hill, you could see the waterfall of colors—gold to orange to red, all the way to plum, exactly like the trees in my parents' yard.

"So tell me," I asked Creed, hoping he'd take me along. "Santos spainges. May does modeling and stuff. What do you do during the day?"

"Well . . ." He grinned. "I would think *this* might give you a hint." He tapped the guitar case—battered and frayed on the outside but like new on the inside.

"I had a feeling, but, you know, I didn't want to make any assumptions." More than anything, I wanted to hear him play again—play for me, like he had outside Hot Topic so long ago. "So, can I come with you?"

"What else were you planning to do?"

I thought of what Santos said, that everyone contributed.

But Creed's expression wasn't angry. If I didn't know better, I'd think he was flirting with me.

"Well, I was kind of thinking of maybe joining Maul and his gang . . ." I teased.

"Not funny."

"Okay, then—I'm getting pretty good at picking up supplies—"

"I heard about the bread train wreck."

"How about getting a job at the Rite Aid? They probably won't kick me out if I can find some clean clothes and don't steal anything." I flashed Creed a smile. "I clean up nice, I promise."

He glanced at me oddly, making me wonder if he was remembering the old *me*, too.

"Where do you come from, Triste?"

Thud. My heart, going into my stomach. I shrugged. "You know. I . . ."

Creed came closer, bumping his arm against my shoulder. The thought of it . . . his skin beneath clothes on the other side of my clothes, my skin . . . made my nerves explode.

"You don't have to tell me, it's just, there's something about you. There's more, isn't there?"

"You saw," I said, pushing the thought of *that night* out of my mind. "Trust me—there's a reason I left."

The scars were almost healed now, hidden under my clothes. All that was left of *her* and what she let herself become.

Creed was staring at me. "Triste?"

Suddenly there wasn't enough wind in the city, enough slope in the hills to contain whatever I was feeling, only that I wanted to run up Madison as fast as I could.

"Come on!" I shouted. Creed was a quarter block behind me now. My hair blew every which way, the air flowing through me with its sunny almost-rain.

Behind me, Creed laughed and started running, too—a gangly, tall kind of running, with his long legs and the guitar thumping, sun rays reflecting honey streaks in his hair.

"Wait a second," he called. "Do you even know where we're going?"

I stopped. Let him catch up. Both of us caught our breaths in front of a bright, graffitied bus stop.

"No," I said, my face close to his. *Alive,* my heart pounded. I wasn't quite alive enough to hold his face in my hands and kiss him. But maybe someday.

"Well, then." Creed took my hand and placed it inside the crook of his elbow. "I'll have to show you."

We caught the free bus downtown and headed toward the nexus of urban commerce, Westlake Center. I knew exactly where the BCBG store was, Betsey Johnson around the corner, Barneys New York. But I had never really noticed all the homeless people hanging around on the steps and napping on benches.

"I have a spot staked out—right outside the front door," Creed said. "I used to play at the food court until security kicked me out. That was a pretty good gig while it lasted. . . ."

I was thinking of the times I'd been here with Jesse and Neeta, before I'd met Asher. I hadn't paid much attention to street musicians before. Not until Creed.

A squawk of crows put me on alert. They chased pigeons away from a sandwich some exec had carelessly dropped. He would never pick it up again, but the homeless crowd eyed the sandwich like it was caviar on a platter. No one made a move as long as the suit was there. Only the crows cackled and dove.

Crows are among the most singularly focused life forms, Asher would say, *creating hierarchies, histories, and their own society through a complex system of communication. . . .*

Watching them made my lungs ache. I needed to get rid of that crow bracelet soon.

"You okay?"

"Yeah—sorry, I was just . . . noticing things I hadn't noticed before."

Creed nodded. We sat down on the steps and Creed started to unpack his guitar. "Hey, we don't have to stay here if you don't want to—I mean, if there's something about this place—"

"No. No, it's nothing. It's just . . . you know. Memories."

"I know what you mean." He played the chord on the guitar. "I think about it every day. The price of doing what you have to do."

"Yeah. Exactly."

He carefully avoided eye contact with me as I watched him tune the strings. "Did you . . . leave something behind?"

He shrugged. "We all did, didn't we? The bad *and* the good."

I thought of Jonah and the Lego car and driver I'd stepped on the night I left. Stench had him now.

It was easier to forget when Creed started to play. His fingers, grimy and ragged like mine, became something more when strumming the guitar, as if the strings themselves were connected to places we'd hidden.

His voice came out deep and soft, like I imagined his kiss would be. He sang a song I didn't know, one about living like waves on top of water, a new current against the depths that had been there for all time. There was loneliness there, and uncertainty, and freedom. All the things I'd been feeling, captured in a breath.

It was the music. His music spoke to my most basic components—nerves, spine, heart.

I wasn't the only one. People had gathered all around us on the steps of Westlake Center. Creed captured them before they could be lost. He was capturing me, before I could be found.

While people dropped change into the guitar case, Creed played another song, and then another.

Later, he bought me an ice cream cone at Molly Moon's— bubble gum, so the flavor would linger after the ice cream melted.

"I should bring you every time. That's the best take I've had in weeks."

My heart jingled along with the coins. "What are you going to do with it?"

"Save it," he said. "I save most of it, whatever I don't have to use for a coat and maybe some new boots." He kicked a stop sign pole, and I noticed the wear on his soles. "That reminds me—you're going to need something warmer. The squat'll be leaky as soon as the rain hits." He paused, deep in thought, as if the weight of our survival were on his shoulders alone.

"Where else would we go?" I asked.

He shrugged, kicking another sign. "Another squat, if we can find one. Though I've been looking and haven't found anything empty. A shelter—"

"*No!* I mean . . ."

"You don't have to explain. When the time comes, we'll find something. Just keep your eyes open, okay? And don't talk to May and Santos about this."

"Why not?"

"They've been through enough. I don't want them to have to worry about it, too."

I savored the last little bit of ice cream on my cone. His—salted caramel—had already disappeared.

I wanted to ask him more, but he stopped short on the sidewalk and took my hand with the ice cream cone.

Slowly, he lifted it to his mouth. Closed his eyes. I wondered if he could feel my frantic heartbeat just by holding my hand. He took a taste and let out a sigh of pleasure. I could feel the echo in my own body.

"Mmmm. I haven't had bubble gum in a long time." He nibbled a bit, releasing my hand. Was he nervous, too?

"Listen," he said. "I don't want you to worry either. Come on."

"Where are we going?"

"You'll just have to trust me."

I did. Far more than he knew.

20

The last of my ice cream cone was gone by the time we reached the Experience Music Project, known as the EMP to locals. The museum, built by Seattle mogul Paul Allen, was an enormous undulating mass of colored metals on the outside and twisted, reflective angles on the inside—supposedly to imitate the rolls and waves of music. It was made from sheets of airplane aluminum riveted together. I knew this because Steven Valen was among the major donors.

But Asher had never taken me there. Music—and any feeling it might inspire—was a mystery to him, and Asher didn't like mysteries. He liked things he could touch. Manipulate. So walking into the EMP with Creed at my side, I felt utterly free.

"Follow me." Creed headed for the entrance. We had to walk through a giant hall of lights and a screen made up of millions of tiny links like chain mail, a vast sheet of armor. The space converted into a dance club for private parties and events, but right now it glittered with a *Matrix*-like stream of colors and numbers.

"Wait, Creed—it isn't cheap to get in," I protested. "I mean, yeah, you had a big haul today, but what about—" He put a finger to my lips as we stood under the raindrops of light. "I . . ."

I couldn't go on. It was all I could do not to fall into him.

"Shhh," he whispered. "Just come."

I followed him to the ticket guy, a music junkie–turned–EMP polo shirt wearer who seemed to light up when he saw Creed. Did they know each other? They shared a low conversation, something about "show" and "gig" and "score," and before I could ask about any of it, the guy was looking over his shoulder and motioning for us to go ahead.

I'd never paid much attention to the hundred-foot guitar sculpture swirling up to the ceiling in the main corridor. But with Creed, it felt like approaching a shrine. There were acoustics, electrics, and basses in every color and shape imaginable mounted on a web of scaffolding, a tornado of instruments like a stairway to heaven. Creed's heaven.

We stood there speechless. And I understood, without him even saying it, that here was the reason he would do anything, go anywhere, to get to the place he was meant to be.

"You'll get there someday," I said quietly, as if anything louder would shatter the connection between man and music.

Something flickered across his face. "Yeah. I hope so."

We spent the next couple of hours haunting the museum like we haunted the streets—sucking every bit of music from every room. The jazz room. The guitar room. The garage rock exhibit. The history of the Northwest scene. Long before Nirvana and Pearl Jam and Modest Mouse, there were Jimi Hendrix, Heart, Ray Charles.

Creed knew more about Northwest music than anyone I'd ever known—all the way down to Oregon and what was on the walls of Icky's Teahouse in Eugene, where tons of bands had come through before getting their big break.

"How do you know so much about Oregon?" I asked, licking the last bit of stickiness from my fingers.

Creed shrugged. "You learn a lot about a place when you grow up there."

I ruminated on this new piece of information, trying to fit it in with what I knew about Creed, which actually wasn't all that much. "I never really pictured you anywhere but here, in Seattle."

"Everyone has to start somewhere. It was Seattle or Olympia for me. Can you picture me in Olympia?"

The only thing I'd ever done in Olympia was attend a state dinner with Neeta and her family—my mom let me have carte blanche at Nordstrom for the most perfect dress—and we spent the entire time flirting with a guy who turned out to be a married campaign assistant. "No, I can't. What's in Olympia?"

"Well, there's K Records, for one thing. And Kill Rock Stars . . ."

"Kill Rock Stars?"

"A record label—then there's all the bands coming out of Olympia. Bikini Kill, Sleater-Kinney, Some Velvet Sidewalk . . . the whole riot grrrl movement, straight edge . . ."

Watching him talk about it, I felt a sinking feeling in my heart. He had something—a passion. A truth. Like Santos and contributing, but . . . more.

My only instinct had been safety. It made me nervous to wonder beyond that. Would Creed see deeper than I wanted him to and be disappointed?

" . . . but I thought I'd have a better chance of making it here." His eyes brightened with the hope of the future, and it broke my heart to think how I could hurt him.

"I . . . I'll help you, if I can," I stuttered. "That kind of dream deserves to come true."

Creed grinned. I hadn't even noticed the tiny chip on the edge of one tooth, whiter than any homeless boy's teeth should be. Even in the squat house, he made sure everyone had a toothbrush. "I have an idea—can you sing?"

"Uh, no."

He grabbed my hand and tugged me toward the sweeping metal staircase. "I don't believe it. You sound like music to me."

His words spread on my skin like sun. "Wait, Creed—seriously, I can't sing. *Can't* is an understatement."

145

He was laughing, still pulling my hand, and the absurdity of it struck me—two homeless kids at the EMP on a date. Was this a date? Maybe, if I could impress him with my vocals. If I could somehow convince him I had a dream as big as his. Outside of Joy's prison, maybe I could find one.

We entered a dark room shrouded in a cacophony of sounds—a preschooler and her parents sampling her voice in one corner; a guy and his girlfriend plucking out "Chopsticks" in another. In the middle of the room stood a giant table where kids and their parents pounded on a huge electronic drum.

Creed pulled me along to the far wall, where sound booths lined up like library carrels under red-tinted lights. Each room came equipped with instruments and the dreaded microphone.

"Oh, no," I said. "You're not dragging me in there."

"I know you—you're being modest."

"No, no, no. No modesty here. Please!"

If I hadn't been fighting for my last shred of dignity, I would have stopped to savor the words: *I know you.*

But he had already dragged me in and shut the door, like we were in high school and hiding out in the janitor's closet. I almost fell into his lap right there with momentum and lust. Somehow, here in this little room with a window, it was different than being on an old, moldy mattress. Naughtier. Real. I put my hands around his waist, threatening to attack.

He slipped out of my grip and spun me onto his lap, grabbing the mike.

"Don't do it!" I giggled. "Save your eardrums! Save yourself!"

"No. Come on. I'll play, you sing." He still had one arm wrapped around me, pinning me into his lap. I twisted until my face nearly brushed his.

I could hardly breathe.

"How are you going to play guitar if you're busy holding on to me?" I was whispering, I realized. Not even able to meet his eyes except through the protection of my lashes. Did I look as warm as I felt?

It took him a second to reply, to shift my weight from one leg to the other. "I hadn't really figured that out yet." He was whispering, too. Eyes still bluer than blue, even under the red lights. "I was hoping you would choose to sing of your own volition. You could be a rock star and not even know it. I could discover you."

His eyes strayed to my lips. I licked them . . . waited . . .

Any second. Oh, God . . .

But he didn't. Instead, a flash of fury passed over his face—almost imperceptible, but still there. He tilted me onto the other knee so he could take the guitar into his arms. "So, um, what should we play?"

It took us a few minutes to figure out something we both knew. He knew pretty much everything indie, and I knew enough not to reveal my limited knowledge of the music scene.

"Okay, let's go for something basic. Like . . ."

"'I Will Follow You into the Dark,'" I interjected.

"Death Cab for Cutie?" His eyebrow rose. "Aha. Definitely Seattle indie."

The truth was I knew it by heart because of Asher. Not because he liked the song, but because he made fun of it—a song about loving someone so much that you would follow them anywhere and make the ultimate sacrifice. It was something Asher would never understand.

"Yeah. Don't laugh! Come on, it's true Seattle. *And* I know the words."

"All right." A grin pulled at the side of his mouth.

"What?"

His eyes softened. "It's just . . . I kind of like that song, too."

He started to play, as if he knew what I'd choose, effortlessly changing the key to my range when I started to sing—not quite alto, not quite soprano, not quite on key.

I knew the words, but the tune was something else entirely. As he plucked out the notes with ease, I sang—no, warbled—the lyrics.

People were standing outside, looking into the booth as Creed ran his hand through his tumble of hair.

It would have been wonderful if I could have stunned him with my singing. And I guess I sort of did.

"It sounds so much better in my head," I offered.

He was trying to be kind, I could see, but it wasn't working. The key, the warbling, the sheer horribleness of it—he couldn't take it anymore, and we were both laughing. "I should have listened. You *are* bad."

"Terrible. I told you!"

"Yes, you did." He snorted. "That was my fault. I should have listened."

"No, wait," I said. "If you want, I can try again."

"No!"

"No, really!"

"Stop. Please."

"But I could be a rock star and not even know it!" I turned around to face him. "You could discover me," I whispered, batting my eyelashes.

He turned red, redder than the lights shifting onto the booth. "Right."

I was wounded. "Okay, then. Show me how it's done, Mr. Rock Star."

He started to play the chords, then the words, singing them like I'd always heard them in my head.

His voice, wispy and gentle and then deep and true, caressed the words as he closed his eyes. *If there's no one beside you when your soul embarks, then I'll follow you into the dark. . . .*

When he was finished, he was holding his breath, too.

Bang bang bang.

"Hey, you've been in there a half hour!" A fanboy hovered outside the window, peering in through his Buddy Holly's.

"Find your pause button!" I shouted through the glass, but the moment was broken.

When we emerged from the EMP, it was colder, and the ice cream boost was wearing thin. "Wanna find food?" I asked.

Pike's Place Market, a dozen blocks away, had rows of fresh produce, cheese samples, even chocolate.

"Yeah—something hot."

I pulled my hoodie closer around me while Creed stuffed his hands into his pockets.

"We could find a corner down here and play for a bit. I could sing." I grinned.

Creed smiled. "That's okay. I figure we should get some food *in* us, not thrown *at* us."

"Hey! Hey, hey. Now that was totally uncalled for."

"So is your singing."

"You called for it."

"Never again." He shook his head. "Never again."

We found a bakery tossing out day-old breakfast sandwiches and made our way down to the park. The wind coming off of the Sound had autumn on its heels.

I must have been so focused on Creed that I hadn't been paying attention to my own breathing. A cold ribbon of air whipped into my lungs and seized me into a long and racking series of coughs. I tried to hold them in until I thought I would burst, remembering the times I had bruised ribs, coughed blood, and stopped breathing altogether.

The emergency inhaler Santos got for me was in the backpack, and I whipped it out for two desperate hits.

Creed watched all of this, first with concern and then with alarm.

"Are you all right? Do we need to go to the hospital?" He

stood there helplessly as I tried to get control, his hand touching my back and neck.

I held up my hand to say no.

"No, I'm fine," I gasped, as soon as I could speak again. "It just happens once in a while, it's not a big deal."

He knew nothing about my history, so he seemed to accept the lie easily. "Where did you get that?" he asked, indicating the inhaler still clutched in my hand. "Santos? Did he get that for you?"

I nodded, and he grunted. "Hmm."

This conversation was going in a dangerous direction. "You were pretty amazing today," I said. "I mean, your music. It really speaks to people." I pulled out my sandwich and thoughtfully popped it in my mouth.

Creed blushed, and even though I meant the compliment sincerely, I felt a little guilty for distracting him.

We walked through the market to a strip of park teetering on the edge of a downtown cliff. Cargo ships and ferries tore through Puget Sound, leaving long white trails in their wakes.

"So what's your skill?" Creed asked.

"Skill?" I thought of street powers—music, disguise, invisibility.

"Yeah. Everybody has one. You need one to survive. I can sing. You . . . "

"Don't say it!"

" . . . cannot. So what is it?"

I thought for a minute. Sacrifice was a skill. I did it with

Asher, sacrificing myself until there wasn't anything left. Now I was sacrificing in another way—my entire previous life gone. But being able to sacrifice wasn't exactly the kind of skill he was looking for.

"I'd have to think about it. But I'd say . . . leaving."

He nodded, as if he knew exactly what I was talking about. "Yeah. That's a talent we've all had to perfect."

We found a place in the park and munched on our sandwiches. "So . . . you came from Oregon and ended up here," I began. The sun was setting behind the Olympic Mountains across the Sound, a smattering of clouds in the sky—the kind of day that made me think Seattle was the most beautiful place on earth.

"Yeah. Olympia's nice, but it's not the same. I'll never get over the water here."

I understood. My suburban home, thirty miles east and nestled in the low, green mountains, couldn't compare. Everything converged in downtown Seattle—the water, the mountains, the sky—and made you feel like you could live outside forever, even if you were under a bridge.

Creed took another bite of his sandwich. "There was this horse I used to know. Callisto—named after a nymph of Artemis."

"Goddess of the hunt," I supplied.

"Yes. She was so beautiful—honey colored, with deep black eyes. She used to love to run on the beach, except she'd always pull toward the water. Over and over again, this would

152

happen. I took her out to run on the beach, and she would try to gallop straight into the ocean."

I realized I wasn't even eating anymore, didn't feel the cold—only the rhythmic gallop of a horse named Callisto. "So what happened?"

"One day I let her."

"You let her go into the ocean?"

"Yeah. I just held on to the reins and let her go wherever she wanted to go."

"And?"

"She kept going. Into the ocean, further and further until she was all the way up to her neck, straining against the water. She didn't swim. She just kept trotting, trying to go where she knew she was meant to go."

Maybe like Creed and his music, straining against the waves. Like me, straining against my asthma and the reins my family and Asher put on me because of it. At some point the horse would have to stop struggling and go back to shore or she would die. But for now, she'd left the reins behind.

"I always think about that, when I think about why I'm here," Creed said.

The sun was almost completely behind the mountains now, except for a sliver of gold. It was so beautiful, I thought I could cry.

21

Santos, Creed, and May had been whispering all day.

"I don't know what you're talking about," May said when I asked what was up. Creed shrugged, and Santos had a big grin on his face.

"What?" I poked Santos, but he danced out of my reach.

It was the day after they'd gone to the New Horizons shelter for a real shower and a change of clothes.

"I'm not going," I'd said.

A hot meal, May promised, even though, according to her, I had a long way to go before I got scrawny. A shower, Creed hinted. New shoes and warmer clothes, Santos promised.

"They talk about Jesus and shit, but the New Ho's are all right. Least, they give decent food," he said. And last week, he'd come home with a jacket, new socks, and underwear.

I thought of my oldest brother, Jesse, the Good Samaritan. He was always the one collecting clothing for the shelters. I'd probably run into my own clothes there, remnants from another life. If they thought I ran away, that would be the first place they'd check. Were there posters up for missing kids? Would they report me to the police?

Even if I didn't, there were other hazards. If I undressed in front of May, she would see the bracelet. And more.

"I can't."

"Oh, come on," Santos wheedled as he ran his hand over Faulkner's sleek fur. "I mean, I didn't wanna say anything, but you're getting kinda smelly—"

"I said no!"

May raised her eyebrows. Santos looked hurt. Creed appraised me thoughtfully. "Fine," Santos said, "you don't have to go . . ."

Creed pushed himself away from the wall. "Leave her alone. If she doesn't want to go, she doesn't have to. We all have things we don't want to talk about."

A sick feeling crept into my stomach. May had things. Santos had things. If they knew about my things, they would kick me out faster than I could swipe a bar of soap from the drugstore. If they knew about my friends, my house, my parents . . . still they wouldn't know a thing about me.

Only Creed knew about Asher, and he hadn't seen the worst of it.

"It's all right, I'll stay with her," May volunteered. "I could help you with your bleach—you got an inch of roots growing out and are starting to look like a fucking skunk."

After the boys left, May said, "I'll go out and get supplies and stuff. You wait here."

"Don't you want me to come with you? It's getting late."

She gave me a withering look. "I'm not afraid of the dark, if that's what you're asking."

"No—that's not what I meant. I—"

"Don't worry about it—I'll get there and back in ten minutes. And seriously, I heard about what happened at the Red Apple Market. I don't want to get kicked out of the closest drugstore." She giggled as she disappeared down the basement stairs. "But thanks for the toilet paper!"

There wasn't much to do, alone in the house. May and Santos had stacks of library books in their room—*A Brief History of Time, Dragon's Keep, Speak, Crime and Punishment*. May had finished reading *Little Women* and was on to *Mansfield Park*. Santos had *The Oxford Companion to Greek Mythology*, opened halfway and splayed across the blankets. They were remarkably well read, I thought, for being homeless.

I picked up *Dragon's Keep* and took it to our bedroom with the candle—nearly burned out. We would need more soon.

Ten pages later, May still hadn't come back. The words started to blur until I was reading the same sentence over and over and closing my eyes, and then I heard the boys coming up the stairs, laughing about some guy at the shelter trying to hang on to his stuff while he took a shower. Everything came into focus again.

Creed stood in the doorway, so huge in the flickering candlelight, all clean and shaved with hair still wet. In a moment, he would lie down on the mattress next to me, so I could bury my nose into him and smell his skin. I smiled as I rolled over.

"Brought you something." He tossed a pair of socks in my direction.

"I fell asleep," I mumbled, reaching for the socks. "Is May back yet?"

Creed's face changed in an instant. "You let her out? What were you *thinking*?"

"Hey, man," Santos interjected from the other room. "It's not her fault—she doesn't know."

Creed closed his eyes with the weight of it. "Herding cats," my mom used to call it when she was trying to get all five of us somewhere at once. Creed looked like he was herding something far more slippery than cats. Ave Rats.

"Whatever it is," I said, "it's not your responsibility. May's a big girl, she can take care of herself." Now I was standing up, a little wobbly. May might have been small, but she wasn't anything like those dead-eyed girls I saw with Maul, or the ones strung out on the sidewalk and sleeping under bridges with their boyfriends. I wished I could be as strong as May.

"You don't know what you're talking about." Creed again.

"I would, if you'd just tell me."

Creed sighed. "You'll probably find out soon enough."

May showed up a few hours later acting like my little brother before a birthday party—hyper and happy and with an armload of bleach and hair supplies, ready to do my hair right then and there. Only it was the middle of the night, and Creed and I were already asleep. Santos was out. We went back to bed, but I could hear her rattling around down below, then pounding down the stairs and into the night.

This morning, she was crashed in the pile of blankets, and Creed wouldn't look me in the eye. The secrets, keeping track of who was carrying what, were starting to become exhausting.

Then Santos came back with coffee and May slept until the afternoon, and suddenly the three of them were whispering and talking about tonight's plan as if nothing had happened.

Now, somewhere close to midnight, the four of us scurried along through the darkened city.

"Where are we going? The Ave?" "The Ave" was short for University Way, a street near the University of Washington where tons of homeless teens hung out. It was another one of my brother's haunts, and the last place I wanted to go.

Santos glanced at May. "No. We don't go there."

I relaxed. We trudged through another neighborhood where I'd been before, north of our usual haunts and much quieter. The houses and yards had more space in between them, and there weren't any brownstones for miles. Every once in a while a car crept by.

"You're gonna love this," Santos kept saying. "It's better than the shelter." Even Creed was smiling, though I saw worry every time he glanced at May.

May was like a shadow of what she'd been last night—tired and tiny, tucking a holey sweater around her. When she caught me staring, she smiled an uneasy smile.

"You okay?" I asked. She looked five years younger just then, a little girl in her five-foot skin.

"Yeah. Fine, thanks." She hurried to join the boys up ahead.

"Right up there," Santos whispered, nodding toward a huge building behind a city park sign: Maplewood Community Center, situated at the top of twenty feet of concrete stairs. The lights were out except for one parking lot lamp.

"You get inside, and I'll keep watch with the girls," Creed said to Santos, who vaulted over the fence and disappeared.

"We're going inside?" I whispered.

"You can't see in from street level," May whispered back. "It's the perfect crime."

Creed's right arm slipped around me as he held up May with the other. His fingers rested on the lower edge of my hoodie, at an exposed slice of skin. I held my breath, wishing for his fingers to find their way under the cloth.

Santos appeared behind the glass doors and unsnapped the locks. "Come on in, mofos," he hooted as we slipped in one by one. He was already peeling off his shirt, revealing a backside rippling with tattoos.

"This way." Santos strolled through double doors and into a vast, echoing room. Only a haze of light came in from the streetlamp, reflecting on an enormous swimming pool. Creed started to take off his clothes as we hit a cloud of chlorine. Santos dove in headfirst while Faulkner padded along the side. May threw the pool light switch, sending a greenish glow up from the water.

I realized I couldn't look at Creed without giving everything away. But I looked anyway.

All the times I'd been wrapped in his body, I'd imagined what he would look like. But I wasn't even close to the real thing. What I'd thought was skinny turned out to be strong and lean. There at the edge of the pool and lit by the liquid glow, it was enough to rouse my every nerve.

"Don't look too hard," May muttered, and I spun around, red and flustered. Part of me, the deepest part, ached with unbearably crazy desire. The rest burned with shame.

I started to unzip my hoodie and unbutton Asher's flannel—I still wore it even though its hold on me was wearing looser and looser. Once upon a time, Asher had made me ache this way, too, before the ache turned into hurt. I slipped the crow bracelet into a pocket before anyone could see.

May stripped to just her baggy T-shirt. She yanked it down to cover herself, but it did nothing to camouflage the bruises on her arms and legs, skinny as sticks. I peeled off my clothes down to my cami and underwear, but no further. There were things I didn't want them to see, either.

160

The boys raced from one end of the pool to the other, cutting through the water and leaving wakes of light. May gingerly climbed down the stairs, as if the pool were a cauldron of boiling liquid.

I dove in and swam as far as I could before coming up in a burst of lungs and water. The farther I swam, the more I could wash off the sweat and grime and burning at seeing Creed.

But there he was, in my path, hidden only by the swirling current between us. I swished to a halt before I could crash into him, and my skin would touch his skin and other places I wished would touch . . .

But instead, he kept a moat of personal space between us, treading water in front of me. "You a diver in your former life?"

Damn. Even the unconscious things could give me away. "No," I said, which wasn't exactly true. I hadn't been on the swim team for years—not since junior high, when one season had landed me in the hospital for weeks with severe pneumonia. Just being here with Creed was a slap in the face of my former life.

His eyes penetrated mine, reading whatever he could, then flickered away, down my neck and wet cami—closer to sheer in the water. The glow of the pool lit up my skin underneath.

"Here," he said, lifting his hands up to wipe under my eyes—black circles were probably running down my cheeks like charcoal tears. I couldn't stop looking at his mouth, wondering what it would taste like. Salty, warm, and maybe a tiny bit sweet.

Under the water, my foot brushed against him, and both of us jumped.

Again, a trace of annoyance flashed across his face—so quickly I wasn't sure if I saw anything.

"You dive like a pro." Then Creed dove under the water himself.

Santos, totally bare, jumped up and down on the diving board. "Watch this! Watch this!" He sprang into a wild sideways dive.

I floated to May, who still waded in the shallow end. Her arms and legs glowed in the aquamarine except for a fresh bruise, circling her arm like a huge hand. Finger marks stood out purple against white.

I gasped. "What happened to your arm?"

She spun around. "Nothing. None of your fucking business," she spat. Two seconds later, she was stalking out of the pool toward the door, her arm held across her body as droplets streamed down her legs.

"May, watch this," called Santos, doing a backward dive. But she wasn't watching. She threw the switch, sending the pool into darkness.

"What'd you do that for?" Santos sputtered, coming up to the surface. Creed was moving toward him.

May came back to the pool and sat down on the side. "I got scared," she said. "Someone's going to see the light." Her face, illuminated by the streetlamp, begged me not to say anything. If Creed knew, he'd be giving someone hell. Me? May? Whoever gave her that bruise? It must have happened on my watch, so it was as much my fault as the person who put it there.

At least, I was afraid that's how he'd see it.

22

"I don't want to go home," May said. She leaned into Creed, who hummed an old REM song I knew: "Nightswimming." Though he gave it a much huskier sound.

The wet underwear beneath my clothes made me shiver. IHOP would be good right about now—my treat, if I'd had any cash left. But I didn't.

"I got an idea." Santos was hopping up and down on one foot, trying to coax a smile out of May. Faulkner's head bobbed up and down from the front of his hoodie. "One word. Bonfire."

A sort of half smile spread across May's face. "Golden Gardens?"

The beach skirted the northwest edge of the city where it

met Puget Sound. Throughout the summer, people flocked there to soak up the six weeks of sun we could count on in Seattle. It would be deserted at this time of night, dotted only with charred remains.

Fifteen minutes later, we were on a west-bound bus—how we were going to pay for it was anybody's guess, but Santos whipped out a ten as we exited at the last stop.

We climbed down fifty feet of stairs to sea level under a canopy of evergreens. At the bottom, white beach unfolded under a crescent moon. My lungs filled with fresh air, like I was being cleaned from the inside out.

Soon Santos and Creed had a fire going. The boys dragged over a bench and knocked it on its side for camouflage. Faulkner kept trying to investigate the flames as Santos drew him back.

Creed leaned against the bench opposite me. After what happened in the water, I didn't trust myself to talk to him.

May shivered, and Santos draped over her like a blanket. He nuzzled her neck tenderly. At first, I didn't recognize the feeling in my stomach, until I noticed Creed watching them with the same eyes. Not jealousy or sadness but . . . longing.

May stared into the flames. "I saw my mom yesterday."

Santos held her tighter and Creed touched her shoulder. May's eyes shifted to me. "I hope she fucking dies out on the street this winter. If not, I might have to kill her myself. Or get Mau—" She stopped herself. Creed sucked in his breath sharply, and I could see he was holding back. What did May have to do with Maul?

"What happened?" I whispered.

Santos tucked his chin over May's shoulder. "You should tell her," he said quietly.

"*You* can tell her, I don't give a fuck," she shot back. Layers of meaning passed between them. Then she relaxed into his arms. "It's okay. You can tell her."

"Her mom is a street mom," Santos said, as if I should know what that meant.

"What's a street mom?"

"She's a fucking drug addict," May muttered.

When she didn't go on, Santos said, "She's like a mom to a bunch of kids up on the Ave."

"Yeah." May huffed. "Not to me. After her boyfriend beat the shit out of me and fucked . . . she abandoned me for the ass-bastard and his stash, and then when he kicks her to the curb, she finds a *new* daughter, a *new* fucking family, a bunch of low-life, ass-sucking Ave Rats—"

May continued muttering and cursing, and I could tell she was on the verge of crying as Santos brushed his lips on her cheek and whispered, "Hey. May. We're your real family. She's nobody. She never took care of you like we take care of you."

Creed's fists gathered up sand and released, over and over.

"What about your dad?" I asked.

"Whoever the fuck he is," May snapped. "Anyway, I'm sick

of talking about me. Let's talk about somebody else. Creed, you tell her your story."

So far I knew almost nothing about Creed. He was from Oregon. He loved music. He was what I wished I could be.

We all froze at the whir of a car. Santos splashed sand on the fire until it simmered down to a low crackle.

"It's not a big deal," Creed mumbled. "Not like May."

May made a *pffft* sound. "We all have our reasons for being here."

Creed shook his head, firelight catching his highlights like the moon bouncing on waves. "It's just . . . it's nothing like May's, so I don't want to pretend I have anything like that," he began.

May rolled her eyes. "Just spit it out, would you?"

Creed was as reluctant to talk as I was eager to listen—every word, every syllable would take me further into who he was. Why he was.

"It's pretty simple, really. My dad's an asshole."

I waited for a May-style retort. *At least you have a dad.* But she was quiet.

"He wanted me to go to school—which is fine. Actually, I'd like to go to school, but not for what he wants."

"Music," I said.

"Yeah. Of course. I always wanted music, and my mom, whenever she would stand up for me—" He caught himself. "My mom, she doesn't really have much of a say."

"She might talk if his dad didn't beat the shit out of her,"

May cut in. "Although if I was your mom, I'd probably keep on talking just so he'd try to kill me and get his ass thrown in jail . . ."

"So you left," I said softly. He escaped while it was still possible, while he was still in one piece. Did his dad beat him, too?

Creed looked at me through his lashes, almost shyly. "I came here to find a new family. And to make music. Music that speaks to people about truth and conviction. What's real."

I wanted to tell him—his first words to me had opened a door, but the music drew me in. I'd known him even before he knew me. Every night when I fell asleep next to him, our connection was much deeper than skin.

All that was left was for our skin to touch.

"I hear it in your voice every time you sing," I said.

Creed seemed close to tears, if that were possible. "I hated leaving my mom—she never stands up to him. Not like I did. She just fades . . ."

Maybe that's why he watched over all of us—because of the ones he couldn't protect, he took care of the ones he could.

"You would never hurt someone on purpose," I said aloud. "Not like . . ." I let my voice fall away. May's brow furrowed, and Santos's gaze rested on me with the force of his whole heart.

"Someone close to you?" Santos asked. "Someone hurt you?"

Concern filled Creed's eyes—and anger, sending a warmth through my body. But he didn't say anything. He would let me tell my own story.

There was only one story I would tell, if I could.

23

"But everyone already knows I'm yours," I'd said to Asher that night.

I was relieved when he finally returned my calls. His silence had been more terrifying than anything he could say.

"You're mine, Joy," he said, when he picked me up in his car, shiny and sleek in the twilight. I could almost see my face in it, the shape of my dread. "Don't ever do that again."

Asher took me back to his apartment and didn't turn on the lights.

Slowly, as if he were seducing me, he took my clothes off piece by piece until I was completely exposed. Only the crow bracelet encircled my wrist, cold against my naked skin.

"I'm wearing the bracelet. I never took it off once," I

pleaded, hoping that all of this—the candles he was lighting, the deliberate way he drew back the sheets on his bed—would begin and end with words only. Angry words, cutting words, words that would reduce me to shame . . . but only words. And then he would take me in his arms and press into me with forgiveness.

His gentle hands, his calculated movements hypnotized me and even sent a thrill into my most secret places. This elaborate ritual had to do with how much he loved me. He wouldn't be so angry if he didn't.

He kissed me hard, so hard that it hurt my lips. Then he put his arm around me and carefully led me to the bed.

The Zippo flashed in his hand, and I frowned at the strangeness of him lighting up a cigarette while in bed.

Instead, he lit another candle and took something out of the drawer—a thin rod that I had never seen before. He spun it rhythmically through the flame.

"I don't care if anyone else knows," he said. "I only care if you know, Joy. You belong to me."

He heated the rod, turning and turning. On one end it had a handle. When the metal glowed, he pressed the handle into my fingers. He was waiting.

I shook my head and pulled the sheet a little closer around me, even though it was sticky hot that evening. "What do you want me to do with this?"

Asher drew the sheet back, exposing the blue veins running around my hip. He put his hand over mine.

"I want you to write."

Gently, he traced the letters of his name with one finger on my hip. The lightness of his touch gave me chills, even with the metal hot in my hand.

I'd read about girls who did things to themselves on purpose, cutting or burning and marking their skin to release the pain of living.

But this was different. He wanted to own me. Not just tag me with a bracelet like the researchers tagged the crows. He wanted to brand me.

He wanted me to do it myself.

"Joy, you know you owe me."

I slowly nodded, tears threatening. He didn't have to say more. He could destroy me, my dad, and my family. If I couldn't find a way to please him, this might only be the beginning.

And all at once, I knew what I had to do.

I could sense the heat, smell the burning of the fine hairs, but I could feel nothing but the shock as I traced the first letter.

A.

I hovered the point as close as I could without touching, only licking the air above my skin, just singeing the surface.

"Closer," he said, reaching toward me.

"No wait, I can do it," I whispered, pushing the metal just a little closer. I might not have heard the sizzle, had I not held back a scream.

Then I seared the letters of his name, one by one. I could see how someone could get addicted to this, trading one kind of torture for another. White-hot pain drowned out the cry of my spirit.

S.

H.

Each letter beaded and coursed with awakening nerves. Asher's face was a mix of fascination and horror. Fascination at my obedience. Horror, maybe, that he *did* have that kind of power over me.

E.

Each line bubbled as the blood began to rush to the surface, inflaming the burns in a rhythmic throbbing cadence. It wasn't just the skin—it was the muscles and sinews and bones beneath, connecting tissues that led to my legs and stomach and heart. Sweat dripped down my forehead, pounding each second out before I burned the last letter.

Then I snaked it into a curve.

Asher's expression changed from fascination to anger in a split second as he knocked the stylus out of my hand. It clattered to the floor.

"You can't even *spell my name* without fucking it up?" he yelled.

He stood up and headed for the bathroom, turning the faucet up to maximum. Suddenly the full scream of my nerves hit me as I tried to stand. *Ice. Water.* My throat was too dry to cry out for them.

"It'll heal," I pleaded, tears streaming down my face. "I'll fix it. I'll try again."

Asher thrust a wet towel into my hand, and I held it against my hip to escape this blackness closing in on my vision. He had a tube of burn salve ready. He wrapped me in blankets and gave me water, maybe to keep me from going into shock. The salve reduced the pain down to a scorched blister. The burn would heal, but it would leave a mark.

Later, after Asher had covered my hip with bites and kisses and had fallen asleep, I ran my fingers over the letters I had made.

ASHES.

He had reduced me to ashes.

And now I would rise.

"Someone close to you? Someone hurt you?"

Santos's question still hung in the air, penetrating the scar tissue of shame I now felt. I'd lied to them by omission because the truth would be damning. If Asher had hit me, I would have something tangible.

But he didn't. He never laid a finger on me, only words. As terrible as they were, as much as they hurt me, they were only words.

Asher didn't hurt me that night. I did it myself.

"Mmm," I responded. I wasn't ready to spill my secrets. As far as they knew, they could be anything—or nothing at all. I wanted to keep it that way.

"You can tell us whenever you're ready," Creed said.

Even May's eyes were wide, as if she could only imagine what would drive a girl like me, 'Burbs, out into the streets to live on shit and garbage and spare change. Santos played with the laces on his shoes, scraping a pattern in the side as if trying to wipe his own memories away.

I could see the kind of force operating here that kept all of them together. At home, they'd clipped my wings and then caged me so I couldn't fall. Here, they bandaged one another's broken wings, helped each other fly. Telling them the truth would expel me forever.

"Yeah, someone close to me," I said, holding my breath.

Creed nodded. He knew this part already.

"Someone beating up on you or something?" Santos asked gently. "More than that?"

Sure. It might as well be. No one would believe that words could be as damaging as fists. I didn't even believe it myself.

"What I saw was bad enough," Creed said softly.

I nodded my head.

Then Creed took me into his arms, the center of gravity and grace. Then they all surrounded me, crying and hurting, bonded not by blood but by pain.

"Fuck," whispered Santos. He cuddled the ferret close to his chest and stared into the fire, as if he were reliving a memory too terrible to speak.

I held my breath. Everyone did, waiting for Santos to say more, maybe tell his story. But Santos only shook his head and let Faulkner go. "Fucking . . . fuck."

No one spoke the question, the one Santos couldn't evade with fast words or fast feet.

But I was different here. I put my head on his shoulder. "Santos."

"Yeah? What up?"

"Where do you go, when you go out at night?"

And right there, I had crossed the invisible barrier.

Creed was unreadable in the smoldering flame. May's face froze. The code on the street was to respect one another's secrets. And here I was, breaking the silence.

Santos stood up, snatching Faulkner out of the sand. "It's fucking cold out here." He didn't once look at me as he gave the sand a hard kick in the direction of the fire. Then he stalked off toward the dock.

"You didn't have to spray us with the damn sand!" May shouted after him. "Now it's probably too late to catch a bus," she muttered. "Somebody's fucking bright idea."

I was hungry and tired and suddenly not remotely able to deal with all of this. I just wanted to get out of here. The moment we'd shared was definitely gone as we trudged up the hill and contemplated the many miles ahead.

Santos started coming back later and later, with deeper circles under his eyes and thinner despite May's offerings of Café Flora pasta and lattes. Wherever he'd been, I didn't ask.

When May returnd from a modeling job, she'd toss out, "It

would be nice if you'd find some way to contribute instead of sitting around on your ass all day."

Creed wasn't even defending me anymore. Instead, he made excuses for May. "She just wants you to make it on the street, you know? It's going to be cold soon, and this house is going to be an ice block."

It was easy to think of all the reasons why he should be defending her. I could think of only one reason why he might want to defend me, and nothing was sure about that. Since we'd been together in the pool, he'd given no sign he thought of me as anything but a sister, and maybe another mouth to feed. He frowned any time he saw me use my medication, but I continued to tell him it was no big deal.

He was right.

I knew what I had to do next.

24

"I don't know about this," May said as we trudged past a row of brownstones in the evening light. "You sure? I mean, they don't mind me bringing an extra girl . . . in fact, Julian got pretty excited . . ."

Julian was May's contact for her art student gig.

"I'm sure." My mom took a life-drawing class once, so how bad could it be? "How did you get into this, anyway?"

"There was an ad up at the school, and I answered it. 'Figure-drawing students looking for models, must be willing to take off clothes . . .'"

"Take off clothes?"

My scar. They would see my scar. And May would, too. "You didn't say anything about taking off clothes."

"Well, of course you have to take off your clothes, numbskull! That's why they call it *figure* drawing—you kind of have to if you wanna draw a figure. You know what *nude* means, right?"

"Yeah, but I didn't realize *nude* and *I* would ever have anything in common in front of a room full of people—"

"They're artists," she shot back. "They don't care about your saggy tits."

"I do not have saggy tits!"

May laughed. "Oh, a sore spot, eh?"

Somebody looked out from a second-story window. Emboldened by May's insult, I shouted, "Mind your own business!"

"Look, you don't have to. You can go back right now and I'll tell Julian you were too chickenshit—but seriously, it's good money, and a free shower, and it's not like you have to f—"

"Yeah, but close enough."

"Fine," said May. "Go back. I'm only taking you because Santos and me think you need a job, even if Creed doesn't give a shit if you sit around eating bonbons all day. *He* can find work for you. But sooner or later, it would be nice if you helped out instead of laying around all the time making moon eyes at Creed."

"I don't make moon eyes," I muttered. "He's like a brother. Like you and Santos, right?"

"Yeah. Right. Just be careful. Don't fuck him over and then

go back to suburbia. If you do, one of us will kill you." When she said it, she didn't look mean or threatening. She just looked scared.

"Santos and I, we got more than sex. He's . . . we look out for each other." May stopped, giving me a look of deadly seriousness. "You watch out for Creed, okay? 'Cause none of the rest of us can. Not like you."

Like me?

But she was wrong—nothing had happened between us since the night we went swimming. We still slept on the same mattress, but instead of curling around me like he used to, Creed was sleeping on the far edge with his back turned to me. When I asked him more about his parents, he responded with stony silence. No. May couldn't be more wrong about Creed and me.

"By the way," she said, "he doesn't want me bringing you here—but don't you dare tell him I told you. I'd have to kill myself."

"Why do you even say that?" I demanded, too annoyed to consider the rest of what she'd said. "Do you even realize how much you talk about killing yourself?"

May rolled her eyes. "God, you're even starting to sound like Creed. I'm just *kidding.*"

"Well, it's not funny. Suicide is not a joke."

"Eff you. Don't go all suicide hotline on me."

We stopped at a U-shaped building, where a tall, skinny guy with buggy eyes and haphazard blond hair let us into a first-floor apartment, weirdly bright after living by candle-light.

"Hey." He smirked, taking May's face in his hands and giving her a wet kiss on the cheek. "You brought her." His creepily round eyes traveled up and down me. I had a bad feeling about this.

"You must be Julian," I replied, crossing my arms over my chest before he could get a good look. It would happen soon enough, I guessed.

He patted May on the ass as she walked in, and she didn't respond—not even to give him the icy stare I'd come to expect. One glare from Creed would send him howling away like a kicked dog. I followed them into the apartment.

A half dozen sweaty boys from goateed freshmen to perpetual seniors crammed into the living room, drawing pads covering their laps. Julian put his hand on May's shoulder as if he was staking his claim. But they knew her, all right. Each of them jerked a cool nod in her direction, then shifted their gazes to land on me.

"Who's your friend?" a chubby guy with a fauxhawk and a lip ring asked. He wouldn't last ten seconds around Maul, who'd shave the hair off before Fauxhawk could scream for his mommy.

May gave me a look over her shoulder as if to say, *Don't mess this up for me.* She wouldn't be half as forgiving as Santos was when I got us chased out of the Red Apple Market—but maybe more forgiving than Creed when he found out I was here.

Julian started to peel her sweater away from her shoulders, but May sidestepped him. "Shower first."

Julian smirked, and the testosterone level in the room notched up toward suffocating. "What about your friend?"

"She gets one, too."

Fauxhawk leaned forward. "Together?"

"Fuck you," said May. She took something from Julian's hand then headed toward the hall. "C'mon, Triste."

I was glad to escape the haze and eyes and imminent detonations in the living room. The tiny bathroom smelled distinctly of boy and brought a rush of memory. My brothers. Poor Jonah. I didn't know which was worse—his believing I'd been kidnapped or that I would leave him on purpose. What would big brother Jesse think if he saw me now?

May turned her back. She rummaged around in her bag and put a pinch to her face, inhaling sharply.

"What was that?" I wasn't even sure I'd seen anything. She turned the water on scalding hot.

"What?" She went back to the business of undressing—holey jeans sagging around her hips, cami and panties three sizes too big. Bones poke out of her chest like toothpicks, held together with razor-sharp collar bones.

"Quit watching me," she barked.

No wonder I looked fat to her. One of her spindly legs could snap in half as easily as a piece of kindling.

The bathroom mirror steamed up as she stepped into the hot stream, and I sat on the toilet waiting for my turn.

"What's taking so long?" One of the guys shouted through the door, amidst hoots from the rest. "You girls don't do anything I wouldn't do."

Suddenly I flashed on Asher's apartment. I always took showers after we had been together, letting the steam blot out my image in the mirror and the water scald me before disappearing down the drain. No one had ever seen me naked except for Asher.

But that was nothing like what I was doing now.

Soon it was my turn. I hid the bracelet in my pile of clothes and maneuvered the towel to cover myself until I got into the shower. The water rained over my skin, washing off one kind of dirt in order to put on another. The heat pricked my scars.

May stood with a towel around her, slathering on concealer. "Get moving. Every minute you're in there is money down the drain."

"I want to be clean on the outside, at least," I retorted. She ignored me, then wiped the steam away so she could line her eyes with black.

Someone pounded on the door. *"Hurry up in there!"*

"Keep your damn pants on!"

May handed me the eyeliner as I wrapped myself in the towel—fluffy but with a faint odor of mildew. "Okay, so you don't have saggy tits." I snorted, and she smiled. "They're going to love 'em."

The compliment made my stomach turn.

When we emerged into the hallway, Julian handed a wad

of cash to May. She flipped through the bills, then handed it back. "This isn't enough."

I felt relieved. I *knew* it wasn't enough for me to take this towel off, no matter how thick the wad was.

"Aw, come on," Julian wheedled. "I added extra for your friend, plus a couple of people aren't here tonight . . ." He gave me a leering grin.

"That's bullshit. Twenty bucks."

Twenty bucks? She was willing to sell us for only twenty more bucks?

"Are you kidding?" I blurted. "Fifty!"

"*Shut. Up,*" May whispered through clenched teeth.

"Forty," Julian said without batting an eyelash.

"Fine, forty," I said. May gave me a look of entirely new appreciation.

Julian went back to the boys to collect more cash.

"They must be desperate," she said to me under her breath.

"Maybe you just never asked for enough."

Out in the living room, the balance of power tilted very slightly with that extra forty dollars. Fauxhawk made some stupid comment about me and May in a raunchy pose, any raunchy pose. May told him to *fuck off,* they weren't paying us enough to do that. Julian gave him one of those nonverbal *shut the hell up* communications, and it was settled.

The guys put on some emo song that would make Creed smash his guitar against the wall, and Julian set up the chipped halogen lamp to cast weird shadows. There was a yoga mat in the middle of the room, clearly only big enough for one of us—or one slim person and another about to disappear.

I watched as May's face went from annoyed to blank. At the pool with Creed and Santos, May swam in her T-shirt, but here, she whipped off the towel as easily as if she'd done it a thousand times.

More money didn't make it any easier for me. The music thundered and moaned, and the boys could hardly contain themselves. They were glad for some fresh meat. Once I let the towel fall, I kept my hand over my hip until Julian snapped, "Hey, can you move that?"

I did.

And there were whispers of *wicked*, and *damn*, and *that's hardcore*, until May glanced over to see what had gotten the boys all riled. Her eyes went wide as they fell on my hip, healed over but still raw and pink.

I didn't speak when we were getting ready to go, or when May collected another ten dollars from Julian, who said, "Bring your friend back next time, too."

We dressed in the bathroom as the emo mix still pounded in my ears. The filthy feeling would be there even if I scrubbed and scrubbed and scrubbed. The eyeliner under my eyes had smeared, but otherwise I looked exactly the same—a phantom, gutted from the inside out.

May didn't say anything when I threw up into the toilet or when I took two huge hits from my inhaler. She didn't ask me about the words burned into my skin. But she knew enough to assume some asshole in my past had done this to me. Little did she know the asshole was me.

When we came out, everyone had left except for Julian and some other guy—not Fauxhawk, but an equally enthusiastic pseudo-artist who shoved his hands in his pockets and kept glancing between May and me and his shoes. Maybe he wanted a closer look at my scar. Well, he was SOL.

I headed for the door without acknowledging any of them. May didn't follow.

Instead, she was huddled with Julian and whispering urgently. *Not this time. Wait.* Her whispers hissed, and Julian was winding up like a spring. The other loser still examined his shoelaces, his legs shaking, like any second he was going to pounce on me as May argued with Julian, in louder voices now. Julian wanted her to stay—no, *both* of us to stay—and they'd pay extra. A *lot* extra, and May could thank me and my negotiating for that. We should be grateful he wasn't calling the police because we'd probably end up with a rap sheet a mile long if he picked up the phone.

"Come on, May, let's go home."

Julian snorted. "Like you two have a home to go to. Sleeping under a bridge these days, May?"

"Get out of here, Triste! Just get out!" May didn't look at me.

The conversation shifted and she started negotiating the terms. "Forget her. Just forget her. So there's two of you. How much money did you say you've got?"

Then I was out the door. I was sick again in the bushes in front of some brick house and started coughing as if my ribs were going to crack.

I had no idea where I was going, only that I didn't want to stay there with her, with whatever might come next.

25

I set out through the dark streets of Capitol Hill. Every shadow formed the shape of Stench, though I hadn't seen him since Creed kicked his ass in the park. But now I felt as vulnerable as the day I'd come.

It was Friday night, so Broadway was hopping. Creed would be here somewhere—playing in the streets or in one of the clubs. His likeliest location was Neumos, maybe White Lava or Chop Suey.

The darkened alley behind Chop Suey flashed through my mind, and my memory shattered like the bottle Asher had broken against the wall. The one piece that remained was Creed, his words imprinted on my mind forever.

I'd found him, but I'd become his responsibility, just like

I had been Asher's, and before that, Jesse's. What I really wanted was not to be a burden to anyone. To be really and truly free.

Santos would be out, too, though I had no idea where to begin looking. I took a breath and strode toward the lights.

The spaingers were out in droves, begging nickels and dimes as the pedestrians went by. One of the girls I thought I'd seen with Maul stood near the exit of the drugstore, smiling at any guy who walked past and sometimes at girls, too. The heavy feeling stayed in my lungs as I thought of what May was doing back at Julian's place. We'd made more money, hadn't we? Why did she think she had to do more?

The whirl of my thoughts almost blinded me to Maul, surrounded by his gang. One of his harem walked up—a new girl not more than fourteen, skinny and freckled and still in clean clothes—and whispered in his ear.

She didn't see it coming, and neither did I. His hand wailed across her face in a blow powerful enough to knock her over.

I felt stunned, as if he'd just hit me. I watched to see if someone would do something—call the police, or at least tell Maul where he could go.

Then, a stranger emotion crept in, a jealousy that shocked me. Everything was so clear for her—didn't she get that? She could walk away, and no one would blame her. Things had never been that simple for me.

But she didn't. It was like nothing had happened, or like Maul had just told a joke. The girl didn't cry. She didn't even react. She just stood up on her freckled legs and whispered into his ear again.

I had to find Creed.

Maul and his gang blocked my route, so I took the alley—cluttered with garbage cans and people too strung out to notice me. It was darkest here, moonlight reflected in puddles I swished through in my sneakers. Water soaked through the holes, and a stray thought flickered through my mind: I would have to ask Santos to get me another pair of socks.

And just like that, I saw his shape in the alley, leaning against a doorway up ahead and lit by the halo of the moon.

"Santos?" I called, picking up the pace. "Santos! I'm so glad you're here."

Then there was someone else.

The figure jumped—both of them jumped. Under the moonlight, with my voice still echoing in the alley, they disappeared into the building like two dark phantoms.

I got to the door, and it was shut tight—maybe the back entrance to some club, locked from the inside.

I pounded on the door. "Santos? It's me, Triste. Are you there?"

"Shut the fuck up!" someone yelled, and an object whizzed past my shoulder. Glass from a bottle exploded on the pavement a few feet away, the label still clinging pathetically to the shards.

"What's going on back here?" A cop or Maul, who knew, but I took off, not stopping to wonder if I really had seen

Santos or if it was some figment brought on by adrenaline. Past the college, past a row of doors streaming with people, past cafés and bars, past the whole, blurry night. The cell phone I'd turned off long ago suddenly felt heavy in my pocket. I could make one call and end all of this.

If only it didn't mean giving up Creed.

I didn't stop until I heard music—mournful guitar chords backed with a hard strum of bass, which spoke to my heart as clearly as if Creed had called my name. I was here, outside Chop Suey. Somehow my feet had known the way even if my brain hadn't. There was no line, only a bored bouncer who took one look at me and shook his head.

"I'm looking for my friend," I said, breathless.

"Yeah, right. That's what they all say."

"No, really. You know Creed?"

"The tall guy? Plays guitar?"

"Yeah. He in there?" My heart pounded so fast, I could've picked up the bouncer and thrown him out of the way. His complacency was infuriating.

He shrugged his shoulders. "He was. I don't know if he's still there."

"I just need to talk to him. If he's not there, I'll come right back out."

He grunted, then let me pass into the steaming club.

At first, I couldn't see anyone—the lights inside were red and flashed around the room at a frenetic pace. My heart matched the bass beat for beat as I looked for Creed. He would be at least a head taller than anyone else.

I thought I saw the guy from the EMP—so this was the show Creed was talking about, the reason the guy let us in for free? I would have to ask him later what kind of connections he had in the Seattle underground music scene. More than I realized.

As I scanned the crowd I saw a face I knew, but it wasn't the one I was looking for.

My pulse went from screaming to slow motion at seeing that face.

Asher.

I started to wonder if maybe it was me who had taken a sniff of something back at Julian's, if I was falling down a rabbit hole and into a nightmare.

And next to Asher was Neeta.

They stood together in the red half-light, looking exactly the same as they did six months ago when we all came here together, like the past and present and future and chaos were all colliding.

All of the air sucked out of the room, my lungs in an iron cage.

The crow charm bracelet seemed to tighten around my wrist. *Little bird.* Unable to fly. The gods of the underworld would recognize me in its grip.

I had nowhere else to go. I spun around and straight into a familiar chest, a body I knew and a soul I wanted to.

It was Creed. I fell into his arms, crying, gasping for air, as if everything in my entire body were breaking.

26

Creed held me tight. His body shielded me from Asher, the club—everything but his own voice.

"Shhh," he kept whispering, into my hair, my ear, my forehead and letting his lips brush against my skin. Relief flooded through me, washing out every emotion I'd experienced in the last twenty-four hours.

He drew me out of the fray. "Come on," he said gently. "Come with me."

I stumbled along blindly toward the back of the room, looking over my shoulder to see Neeta and Asher in the crowd. Were they alone? Asher looked angry. Intent. Gripping Neeta's arm as if he owned her already. She was my innocent friend, too smart to get involved with someone like him. What was

Neeta thinking? Would he do to her what he'd done to me?

Creed led me through a back door I never knew was there, into the alley where a trailer balanced on cracking cement blocks. In the moonlight, I emptied myself of air and took two desperate puffs of my emergency inhaler, then coughed until I thought I would throw up.

Creed's arm still held me close as we got into the trailer, lit by a small, olive-green lamp. There were chips all over the floor, empty beer and water bottles littering the counter. He settled me onto the dilapidated couch, which smelled like sweat and booze but felt comforting and warm with Creed there beside me.

When my sobs had subsided, he gently put his finger under my chin. I'd been hoping and waiting for this all along, but now that it was here, I couldn't believe it was happening.

His heartbeat pounded slow and steady beneath my hand, the wire between us as taut as a guitar string. I ached for it to break.

My breath came out in ragged wisps. We were totally alone in the trailer, no air but our own breathing, the music muffled by the door and floating into the trailer like a mist.

He watched me. Gauged his moment. Could he feel the tightness coiled inside me, waiting to be released? "Triste." The way Creed said my name, it sounded like a prayer. "Triste. What happened? Why aren't you with May? Where were you?"

I didn't trust myself to answer. Not when we were here on this couch together, when I wanted him so badly I could taste it. His eyes lingered on me.

And then the story came rushing out in a flood—how I wasn't contributing, how I'd gone with May to Julian's, how I'd left her there, or maybe she had left me. I couldn't tell anymore, only that I couldn't stay. I *couldn't*. And I told him what Maul did, and how I saw Santos in the alley, only I wasn't sure it was Santos, and he'd left me alone and afraid and I'd run to the club and right into Creed.

But I'd left out the most important part: seeing Asher.

After what I told them on the beach, I knew what Creed would do if he saw Asher out there now. He had already fought for me once and would do it again if I asked.

The scene played out in my head, half dream, half nightmare: Creed storming out of this trailer and into the club with one thing on his mind. He was going to kill Asher.

And I wanted it.

No, I didn't!

Because then Asher would know I was here. I would have to go back. . . .

No.

The scars burned under my clothing. The bracelet closed in on my wrist, as if it knew Asher was only a hundred feet away. As long as I had it, he would have some kind of hold on me.

Creed said nothing, but I could tell his body had a coil in it, too, another kind of desperation and desire. "So May is still at Julian's?"

"Yeah, I think so."

His lips pressed together in a thin line.

"Creed," I said softly, "do you want me to stay?"

His lips parted. I could feel his heart thudding against my chest. He was so close.

"Creed!"

Pounding on the door almost made me jump out of my skin, and Creed pulled away as if I'd burned him. A round guy with a couple days of beard popped his head in. "Oh. Uh, sorry. You're on in a couple minutes."

Creed nodded to him, then turned to me in one awkward motion. "Yeah, I'm supposed to be playing with the band tonight. It's pretty cool—they're looking for someone to play with them for local shows . . ."

The rush in my ears made it hard to hear. Hiding out in this trailer with him, I could pretend none of this was happening. He hadn't almost just kissed me.

"You wouldn't want to come watch me, would you? There's a backstage area behind the curtain, so you could hang out there . . ."

Asher was still out there. So was my best friend.

"You can see the stage and the crowd," Creed was saying. "Nobody will be able to see you . . . "

He wiped a tear from under my eye then led me to the wings. I was cloaked in darkness, safe for now.

Creed was in his element, with a borrowed electric guitar across his stomach and his fingers finding the melody.

His voice flooded the microphone like warm liquid reaching deep into my parched and frozen body. It wasn't the words he said but the way he said them, as if everything in his heart were pouring out, expansive and beautiful and true and touching me in the place I wanted him to know but couldn't show him.

For him, that place was here, on the stage, making music.

And suddenly I could see what his future held, where his path was headed.

He already knew his first love. Why would he need me?

27

That night when Creed wrapped his arms around me before falling asleep, I made myself turn away. May came in later. Santos didn't come in at all.

The next morning, I found Santos downing his coffee and feeding nibbles of day-old bagel to Faulkner. "Hey," I said, my mouth moving like cotton. "Were you—"

"Where's Creed?" he cut me off.

"I don't know. He wasn't here when I got up."

That's when I remembered. Today, I had a mission.

"Hey, Santos, I need your help with something. Know any good pawn shops?"

Santos and I headed to Pioneer Square, the oldest part of Seattle, where Gold Rush–era buildings competed with shiny new high-rises and the homeless population nearly out-weighed the normals. "Never go to the same place twice," he advised. "There's plenty of shops, and the last thing you want is to be remembered."

When we got to the shop, I slipped him the bracelet. "Holy effin' eff-bomb," he whispered, dangling the white gold chain. It would be worth more in the Tiffany box, but this is what I had.

The crow taunted me with its ruby eyes. I was glad to get rid of it—to get rid of Asher's hold on me—for good. Hopefully it wouldn't be a cursed item coming back to haunt me, like the crows that still dive-bombed the UW researchers generations later. Santos examined it more closely, reading the *Little bird* label on the plate. "Yeah, I can get you good cash for this."

I waited outside and tried to blend into the scenery. Anyone could identify me—the girl with white-blue hair and black eyes—even if no one knew my name.

Afterward, we walked down to the waterfront. "I wanted to ask you," I began nervously. "Did I see you out last night? In the alley?"

Santos looked away and shrugged, his face unreadable until I saw his hands—brown and wiry, veins popping with what-ever he was hiding. "Maybe. I was spainging up on Broadway."

I gave him a narrow look. "I walked most of the way up Broadway and didn't see you—I saw Maul, though."

"Yeah. Asshole," he muttered, confirming the feeling all of us had about him. "I saw him, too."

He walked faster, but I kept pace.

"I didn't see you there."

"Maybe I was taking a leak in the alley or something." Puget Sound stretched out below us and sent fishy wind into our faces.

"I went through the alley to avoid Maul," I said. "I was there. I saw you."

Suddenly Santos kicked a giant blue mailbox, causing the crowd around us to leap backward. "You didn't see shit! Just leave it alone, okay?"

I staggered backward. Creed was right. There were secrets we kept, even from family.

We made our way back to Broadway without saying much. I'd almost forgotten the pawn shop when Santos reached into his pocket.

"Okay, so—you're not going to believe this!" He stopped, right there at the Pine Street crossing, and handed me a huge wad of tens and twenties. "They gave me almost three hundred friggin' bucks for your bracelet! Which means, that's like a *quarter* of what it really costs. Where the hell did you score that?"

"Um, somebody gave it to me." My wrist seemed so much lighter now that it was gone. The cash didn't feel so heavy, since I knew exactly what to do with it.

"If somebody's just giving you something all dope like that, I don't get why you hang out with us."

I pondered the question. "Well, why do *you* hang out with *us*?".

"Better than being a *ward of the state*." He said it like it was a title, no better than *trash on the street*. "Obviously you've never been in foster."

I shook my head.

"Then you're lucky."

"What's it like?"

Santos whistled. "I lived in, like, ten places in two years—none of them good. It's like child slavery, that's what it is. Fucking child abuse. And the worst part is they'll move you or send you back to your shitty parents in a heartbeat. I'd rather live in the pit of hell with my street fam than get lost in that shithole ever again."

The smell of Dick's french fries wafted in our direction. Usually Maul and his gang hung around outside the stand, but I didn't see them today. Faulkner stuck his pink nose out of Santos's hoodie to take a long whiff.

"Man, you're lucky I didn't charge a finder's fee," Santos wheedled. "Otherwise I'd be going over there and buying myself an ass-load of those fries."

I smiled—I was forgiven, I hoped. "Come on, I'll buy you some."

A half hour later, Santos and I were munching on our fries and climbing through the hole under the stairs. That's when we heard the yelling.

"*What the hell were you thinking?*" Creed shouted. "What

did you *think* they wanted?"

May's voice came back shrill and quavering. "She's been sitting around on her ass all day and doesn't do a fucking thing to contribute!"

A pause.

"She wanted to *do* something, Creed! What the hell is your problem? You don't *own* her."

Something crashed.

"You don't own any of us!"

Boots stomped across the floor. "You had no right."

"Fuck you! Just because you can't protect your *mom* doesn't mean you can control the rest of us."

I followed Santos up the stairs and burst into the kitchen, but the yelling had stopped.

We found them in the living room. Creed crouched over May, who curled into a tiny ball on the couch, eyes puffy and red.

"What's going on?" Santos demanded. "You're going to alert the whole neighborhood."

"Creed thinks he's my fucking *parent*," May sniped.

I knew what this was about. It was about me, and what had happened last night at Julian's.

"Creed, listen," I began.

"What?" he exploded, and I realized I'd never seen him explode at anything. Ever. "You're gonna tell me you wanted to strip for a bunch of losers and then fuck them afterward? That's what you wanted?"

It was like he'd hit me. Like Asher's words used to. I felt a burning in my throat. "No!"

"Then what?"

Now was the time.

The wad of cash bulged in my pocket. I whipped it out and tossed it in the middle of all of us—dollars fluttering to the ground in a heap while everyone watched the pile breathlessly.

"Oh my God," May said.

Whatever they had been arguing about came to a full stop.

"Where did this come from?" Creed demanded.

"It doesn't matter where it came from—it's my contribution."

They were too stunned to say anything, too mesmerized by the pile of money to care.

"Maybe for once we can eat something that doesn't come from a garbage can," I said wearily.

"I get at least half," May said, when she found her voice again. "I've been floating her for weeks."

Santos: "No fucking way—I've been taking her all over the place, getting her socks, and teaching her how to live out here."

Creed: "Santos—what did you do? Where the hell did she get this money?"

Santos started to backpedal, and the argument took off in a totally new direction with all three of them going at it.

It's her contribution!

You *brought her here, she's your responsibility.*

You should have told her she couldn't just squat here from the beginning.

She owes us.

Wait, everyone, just wait.

"I'm done with this," I said.

They were still fighting when I went to the bedroom. Arguing over me. May's voice was high pitched and birdy, Creed's like the thudding of a bass line and Santos interjecting. The words disappeared into a blur of sound as I lay down on the bare mattress and watched the dust particles rise in the air. Moldy sharpness pricked my nose, the hazards of living in a leaky squat house. The black fuzz growing in damp corners was starting to affect me.

I took a long breath of my inhaler, then swapped it out for a new one. The weight of everything pressed on my chest.

Fatigue overtook me, and I lost track of the discord below until something sharp and loud startled me. A door banging?

Then male voices—not Creed's or Santos's.

I almost choked on the air. More shouting followed a slow crack, like bones bending and then breaking.

A scream—May? May was screaming. What was happening?

"Creed?" I called down the stairs.

"No!" someone yelled amidst a scuffle. Something hit the wall with a sickening thud.

I had to will my feet to move—down the stairs, over the rotted boards to where I could see into the living room. It wasn't Creed and Santos at all.

I thought getting rid of the bracelet would free me from a curse—instead it only brought a new one.

Oh my God. How had they found us?

Maul and his gang filled the living room—and Maul had Creed pinned to the floor.

28

The living room was in total chaos. A bloody clump of fur lay in a heap by the wall, not moving. Maul held Creed down while one of the others punched Santos in the stomach. Another gripped May while she kicked and shrieked. Money was everywhere—under Creed, on the floor. A thin girl with stringy brown hair—the one Maul hit?—was gathering it, dollar by dollar, into a wilted stack.

"Ah—look who's here," Maul said when he saw me. A chill crawled over my spine. Had we led him here? The thought made me gasp with fear.

"I told you," he said softly, "you should have come when I asked nice. Now you're gonna have to be broken first."

"Stay the fuck away from her!" Creed shouted—he was

206

all arms and legs and wiriness, trying to get up off the floor like an overturned crab, but he was no match for Maul's sheer bulk. Maul raised his fist and brought it down hard against the side of Creed's head. I felt the pain in my gut.

Before I knew it, I was charging—straight for Maul, like a ninja warrior girl ready to kick him in the head. Someone came out of nowhere and caught me midjump, but the surprise of it was enough to knock Maul off balance. Creed wriggled out from under him and picked up a board from the mess of shrapnel on the floor.

Wham. It hit Maul's head with a terrible crack.

He staggered from the blow, but he was like a tree struck with only a branch. "You shouldn't have done that, *Creed*."

The guy holding me tightened his grasp, pressing the chains on his jacket into the grooves of my spine. I suddenly felt numb, like my brains were rattling right out of my head. A blast went off above my ear and into my eye, my skull, my jaw. He'd hit me. Blackness gathered at the edges. Any second I was going to pass out from the shock. My vision became a shaft of light and sound, spinning.

Creed was watching me. I held his gaze to force the darkness away, even though I was feeling a warm trickle now through the explosion.

Don't let go, his eyes said to me. I listened.

Vaguely, I made out Santos wrestling with some other Maul rat and screaming *puta madre*, but even his dexterity couldn't help him escape. May went limp as a rag doll in the arms of her captor. Maybe she wasn't even trying to get free anymore.

Maul's raggedy girl finished picking up the money, all that was left of Asher's hold on me. Maybe it was better to get rid of it entirely.

"You can have the squat," I heard someone say. "Just let them go." It was Creed. Still trying to protect us, even when he was utterly helpless.

Maul laughed—a wicked cough. It made the thrumming in my brain constrict. "Yeah, we'll take the squat, but you're not gonna get off so easy." One more violent blow and Creed was on the ground, holding his head. The pain in my own became the low roar of panic.

"That should hold you for a while." Maul sauntered over in my direction. "You think you're so tricky. Yeah, it's going to be fun breaking you, invisible girl."

I resisted the urge to bite off his finger. The liquid from my forehead rolled down to my chin and dripped onto the floorboards.

"Your hair is pretty. Did May do that for you?" Maul's voice was like a rusty nail scraping my skin softly. "She's good at that." He laughed. "There are so many things May is good at. Or maybe you didn't realize. Maybe she's turned over a new leaf, hanging out with you posers. Especially you," he spat in Creed's direction.

Creed was still on the floor—knocked out? Planning an attack? I couldn't tell. There were four of us and five of them, but one was just the girl. I knew she wouldn't put up much of a fight. The others, each of them pinning one of us, were as big as Maul.

Maul touched me on the cheek. "May only comes to me when she wants something now—which is more than you realize, Miss Sunshine. I'm not so sure I have her loyalty anymore, now that you're here."

"Are you for real?" May's voice sounded hard, like the night I first met her. Sarcastic. One by one, she lifted the guy's arms off of her haughtily while he let them drop to the ground. "I'm through with these dipshits. In fact, you can have the fucking house—I'd even stay with you."

"May," Santos warned.

"Shut the fuck up, Pantsos! I'm sick of your fucking self-righteousness when you are *so* full of shit it's not even funny. You're as bad as Creed. You make me *sick*, that's what you do. So don't even try to boss me around."

Through the thick tunnel, I saw Santos's face—the pain rippling in my head reflected in his eyes.

"What are you doing, May?" It was my voice, small and insignificant.

May snorted. "Now that's funny, 'Burbs. You sticking up for someone besides your own pathetic fat ass."

She turned to Maul, who was watching her with a grin, and gave him a slow, deadly kiss. "Please tell me she's not going to stay. She's got to be the most annoying fucking person I've ever met in my life. If she stays . . . seriously, Maul, you've gotta get rid of her. She's a damn parasite."

He kissed her back, hungrily, and then smacked her across the face. Hard. "Don't you tell me what to do."

A shiny mark bloomed on the side of her face, but it only seemed to up her level of cheek. "You want me to stay? Then get them outta here."

Creed was rising from the floor, barely steady on his knees. "May . . ."

"You shut the fuck up, *Creed*! You're the biggest hypocrite of all of us. You think you're protecting us when you can't even protect your own *mother*. She's there and you're here, pretending like you're the savior on the white horse and leading everybody like you're Jesus Christ himself and screwing with everybody's emotions. You can't even tell the truth because you're too scared. What kind of asshole does that?"

Creed's jaw dropped open like she dealt him a physical blow.

May dragged Maul toward the stairs with a look I recognized—the same face I'd seen on Maul's girls when they camped out on the streets, pouting and smiling. Was it fake or was it real? Every time she left the house, Creed and Santos had worried she would come back high or worse. *She has a history with Maul,* Santos had said. Now I was seeing it firsthand.

Maul's gang stood around like they weren't quite sure what to do with us. The stringy girl leaned against the wall like she was glad it wasn't *her* walking up those stairs.

"Maul, what do you want us to do?" the guy holding Santos shouted.

Maul and May turned the corner into the bedroom with the mattress—the one I had slept on with Creed for the last two months. Now it was gone. Everything as we knew it, gone.

"Get them out of here!" Maul roared. A muffled giggle followed.

"Here, take your shit with you," May called down the stairs, scooting Creed's guitar case around the corner with her foot.

Maul's hand landed across her face, knocking her head against the wall with a crack. "What the fuck do you think you're doing?"

"Sorry, I—"

"Any of you guys need a guitar?"

The gang grunted. The stringy girl looked up like she wanted to speak. Whatever she wanted to say was lost, because in one swift, merciless movement, Maul opened the case and kicked its contents down the stairs, where it bumped and cracked and finally splintered to a stop.

Creed and I were still staring at the pieces of the guitar when Santos gripped our arms. "What the hell are you waiting for? They're letting us go!"

Sounds of muffled laughing and moaning floated from the bedroom like dust particles, past the stomach-wrenching smell of the shit room and the torn-out kitchen and the rickety stairs leading down to the basement and out of the abandoned house I would never see again.

May's voice trickled after us, and I finally knew her street power.

She just used it to betray us all.

29

With Creed between us, Santos and I dragged him somewhere—anywhere—to recover from Maul's brutal beating.
His mouth had stopped bleeding, but now a black bruise
spread relentlessly across his jaw. Where would we go now?

My head was still throbbing from the blow, but it didn't
feel half as bad as Creed looked.

"I'm telling you," Santos said, "we should take him to New
Ho's. He can hang out there for a while—they have a doctor—"

"No," Creed moaned. "We're not going to the shelter."

"What the fuck?" Santos tripped and almost lost his grip
on Creed, who was as heavy as Santos and me put together.

"No." Creed coughed like one of his lungs had collapsed.

Fresh blood trickled from a cut on his lip. "Triste," he croaked. "She won't be safe there."

"Fuck Triste, man! You need help!"

"Creed, listen to me," I said, hoping he couldn't hear the desperation in my voice. "I don't have to go. Santos can take you, and I can wait for you. I can hang out . . ." Where could I hang out? Did I still have the power to hide in plain sight, now that so many enemies had seen me?

"Maybe you should go home," Creed whispered.

I ignored him. It wasn't even about home anymore. Now it was about him. Going home would mean losing him forever.

No. It would take far more than getting kicked out of the squat to tear me away. "*You* could go the shelter, at least for a little bit. I can take care of myself."

I looked at his hands, the same ones that had gently strummed his guitar and wrapped around me only hours ago. They were shaking, as if everything was crumbling in his grasp.

"That's all I need," he sighed. "First May, then you."

"Fuck May." Santos's voice ripped through the rainy air with a sob. "She can go fuck herself, if she wants to stay with Maul instead of us. She can . . ." His voice trailed off, piercing the exact same feeling lodged deep inside of me. What did she think she was doing? Maul didn't care if she lived or died. Didn't she know that?

"She did it for us," Creed said quietly.

Santos spat on the ground, looking away—but not before

I saw the tears he was trying to hide. Faulkner was dead. His best friend, his family, had betrayed him. "That's propaganda, and you know it. She's been sneaking off and tripping with him for weeks now. Maybe you haven't been paying attention. You've been too busy trying to shake the house with Triste here."

Creed said nothing, only closed his eyes—from pain or embarrassment, I couldn't tell. Nobody knew better than I did how wrong Santos was.

But Santos wasn't finished. "For all we know, May led him right to us."

"Stop it!" Creed shouted, before falling limply between us.

When we got onto the bus headed downtown, people made way for three misfits soaked with rain and broken in spirit. Santos sat on his own bench while I huddled with Creed, trying and failing to keep him warm. The shiver was spreading now as I held him, hair streaming with blood and tears.

The shelter was only a few blocks away from the Space Needle and the EMP where Creed had taken me. It seemed so long ago now—even the crazy bright colors and metallic shrine for all things musical looked grey under the autumn sky.

There was a crowd already forming outside the shelter— kids I'd seen on Capitol Hill and others I hadn't, some of them looking like fresh meat. Plump and clean, wide-eyed at the fighting and tripping and the great cloud of smoke rising above the group. Had I looked that naive when I first came?

You could tell who the volunteers were, even though they

tried to blend in with their thrift-store clothes and unassuming posture. An adult in a flannel shirt and jeans came over. He looked like he'd seen a fair amount of shit. One of his eyes wandered every which way behind his rockabilly glasses, like it had almost been knocked out of his head and now kept searching around for a place to stay put.

"Hey, Ron." Creed nodded to him, struggling to stand up on his own. I hid my face before the guy could get a good look at me.

"Hey," Ron said. "How's the music?"

Creed shrugged. "Going okay." Creed was a terrible liar. Ron just stared at him, his crazy eye wandering. He was like a cyclops. Nothing much was going to get past him, I could tell.

"You're so full of shit," Santos said, punching Creed in the arm. "Hey, Ron. You're not gonna believe the shit that's happened to us today." And Santos launched into his way of fast talking while the guy listened. "Maul . . . and beat the shit . . . Creed knocked him on his ass . . . .and the guitar is smashed to smithereens . . . kicked out of the squat . . . and now he's totally fucked up." Everything but what happened with May.

But Ron had to know something was up, because here were Creed and Santos with me instead of May. The three of them were inseparable.

"Sandy's inside with clean clothes and food for the girls," Ron said to me. "You can get in line right over there. She can clean you up, take a look at that cut."

I swiped at the side of my face and came away with a trickle of blood. "Uh, thanks." How many seconds would it take for someone to recognize me from my old picture?

I wanted to stay with Creed, but there was nothing I could do for him now.

Santos must have read my thoughts. "Don't worry, I'll take care of him."

The eye wandered toward me and I shuddered. That eye could see things. I had to get out of there now.

30

I went back to Capitol Hill. It was dangerous but familiar. I knew where not to go to stay out of Maul's way. Avoid Broadway, no question—he'd be hanging there and his girls would be out attracting a catch for the night. I shuddered to think of May. Would she be out there, too, or would Maul keep her as his own?

You want me to stay? Then get them outta here.

The hurt was so mixed in with the shock, I remembered every word. She wanted to die—she said it all the time. Was this her way of finishing the job?

The only thing to do was go where Maul would never go.

The church behind the community college was lit up like a Christmas tree. It was Sunday night, Jesus break for churches across the country. My brothers and I had been to church a thousand times, hearing about homeless disciples who wandered around healing the sick and raising the dead.

Those were powers that could actually do something on the street.

There was construction going over in the next lot—almost finished now, and suddenly I realized it had the same New Horizons logo on a sign: FUTURE SITE OF TEEN TRANSITIONAL HOUSING SHELTER.

Damn. These people were everywhere.

If I stood close enough to the brick wall of the church, I could avoid the steady trickle of rain. A fierce cough enveloped me. The hood of my sweatshirt wasn't quite enough to keep the dampness and cold from soaking in, but it was enough to shield me from the stream of church people heading in and out of the side door while I curled up for the night.

Creed would be okay, I told myself. He was almost standing when I left. Santos was talking Ron's ear off, each story more outrageous than the last. Stories were the currency of the street even if truth wasn't, and Santos had an abundance.

A woman came out of the church—a mom type, short with a rounded face and haphazard greying hair—and uncloaked me with one glance.

"Do you want to come in?" she asked with a smile—an irresistible one that would be my undoing if I let it.

I shook my head and coughed. "No, thanks."

She nodded. "Well, if you decide to stay, there's soup and

cookies inside." Now that she mentioned it, I could smell tomatoey warmth wafting from the open door. She lingered, presumably waiting for me to change my mind. Ron, this church lady, they were the kind of people who would lure me out of invisibility and lead me straight back to what I'd left. *No, thank you.*

A few minutes later, she came out with a napkin bundle and a steaming cup. The napkin was full of cookies—chocolate creme sandwiches, Jonah's favorite. The cup was full of minestrone and smelled so good I could cry.

I gobbled down the soup and cookies, but she wasn't leaving yet. My mom would have swept in, dropped off the food and backed out gracefully by now. This mom stood there watching me with a crow's gaze.

"There's going to be a shelter here soon, across the street. Do you know about it?"

I nodded. "Uh-huh."

"But until then, there are a couple in the U District and another not far from here."

I slurped the soup, waiting for her to finish and go away. "Thanks."

"You could wash up here, if you want. There's a bathroom at the end of the hall."

Real plumbing—now that was a draw.

I followed her into the building, twenty degrees warmer than outside, and she stopped at a wooden closet for a taupe-colored puff of fabric that looked more like a potato than a coat. "You can have this, too. The bathroom's right there."

Everything about this was so familiar and almost comfort-ing, turning the other cheek and wondering what Jesus would do. I knew he came to set the captives free.

After escaping the cozy seduction of the church, I huddled outside an apartment dryer vent. The coat was roomy enough to curl up in, with a secret pocket to stash my phone and the one inhaler I'd managed to grab before Maul and his gang showed up.

I fell asleep to the sounds of shouting and sirens and the heady scent of Snuggle freshness, reminding me of J3 and how he would creep into my room after he'd had a bad dream and fill my nose with a mix of sweaty hair and fabric softener. We had clean clothes on Tuesdays and Fridays, like clockwork. Even our laundry served to confine us.

A crow cawed from a swaying phone cable, depositing his filth before dive-bombing a bit of something on the road. *But things have changed,* I silently told the crow. *I've changed.*

Some of the homeless jumped trains and migrated, I knew. But it would take hundreds of miles and dollars to go where I would never be found. Where *we* would never be found—me and Creed and Santos. May? She'd made her choice to live with the bad guys instead of die with the good. Maybe she was choosing death either way.

When I awoke, I went back to the New Ho's shelter. It was early enough to watch the red skies of dawn, portent of another stormy day.

Creed sat alone on the curb, his arms held in guitar stance. Without it, he looked like a shadow, pantomiming his former street power. To see part of him missing brought tears to my eyes. I held back another cough.

He hardly recognized me in the potato coat, but when he did, he looked relieved to see me. "Where did you get that?"

I grinned as I sat down next to him. "Some church lady."

"Giving out free coats? Sign me up. Maybe they've got a spare guitar." He laughed, a lame attempt to cover the hole left by its absence. "Or you could start singing with me. Because you know people would pay good money to hear someone whose voice is on such a sucktastic level—*ow!*"

He recoiled from my fake punch and rubbed the spot on his ribs. He could fight Stench by himself, but facing Maul and his entire gang was a different matter.

"You okay? Anything broken?"

He shook his head, and I noticed how clean he was— shaved and soapy-smelling. He looked better after a night in a real bed. "Nah. The doc said I just have a couple of bruised ribs—bruised eye, bruised jaw, bruised hand, bruised ego . . ."

He showed me his hand, the black and purple on his knuckles spreading out toward his fingers. "At least I won't have to play for a while, because this hurts like a bastard. Come on, let's get out of here."

We walked for a few minutes without talking before I realized we were missing something. "Where's Santos?"

Creed tucked himself further into his army jacket. "He left."

"He left you? After Maul beat the crap out of you?"

"Well, it wasn't crap, exactly—"

"Where did he go?"

"Working."

I coughed in disgust. "What the hell?"

"Crap? Hell? You're getting so daring with your expletives these days."

"Shut up!"

"I'm just saying. So where did you spend the night? At the church?" He was resisting a smirk.

"No! No way. Outside someone's dryer vent, actually. An apartment building."

The smirk turned to a frown. "You can't do that. It's too dangerous. Someone could find you and . . . I don't want to think about what someone might do to you. We could go to a shelter. You could stay here, Triste—it isn't state-run, they don't ask questions. No one's going to turn you in, no one's going to—"

"How do you know that? You don't even know what I'm running from." As I said it, I felt the guilt tingling at the fringes of my consciousness and pushed it away—I wasn't even certain myself sometimes. "Why is it so dangerous for me? As if Santos going off in the middle of the night isn't? Tell me that."

"It's different."

"Why is it different? Where does he go? What would you

tell me, if you could?"

"You can't ask me that."

"Why not?"

"Because."

"Because why?"

Creed stopped in the middle of the street. Downtown was waking up—cars darting here and there on the maze of one-way streets in Seattle's mass of transit confusion. The smell of fresh coffee wafted from a Starbucks with normals darting in and out of the early morning mist. Creed stared at me, a world of truth in his eyes.

"Because I don't ask you to tell me everything. I trust you. And I'll protect Santos no matter what." He leaned in closer, close enough for me to feel his breath on my lips. "Just like I'll protect you."

31

Creed didn't ask me about shelters again, but finding somewhere safe to sleep was foremost on both our minds. Besides, the shelters would separate us, boys and girls. And I didn't want to be separated from Creed again.

There weren't many other options. Music and invisibility weren't much help when it came to finding someplace warm and dry. We staked out new possible squats, but it could take weeks or even months for us to find something without a prior claim. Abandoned buildings were hard to come by unless you had a gang to fight for them, and we were down to just three people—sometimes, just two. There were bridges to sleep under, parks until we were chased out by cops, Dumpsters behind buildings—all of them soaked with the relentless Seattle rain.

My cough was getting worse. When I couldn't mask it any longer, Creed accepted my explanation—I told him I had a cold, which was common enough on the streets. Besides, he was focused on looking for somewhere to live. Spainging enough money to get a carton of french fries here, a muffin there. Avoiding Maul, who could change his mind and hunt us down. Stench was back on the scene and grinned at me from afar with my old backpack on his shoulder. He seemed to sense the tilt in his favor.

We saw May on the streets one evening as the clouds threatened to burst. She looked thinner and yellow. Bruises? Drugs? She pretended not to see us as she strutted past in a new jacket and pants hanging off her hips.

Before Creed could stop me, I called her name.

The heels of her boots clicked to a halt. She spun around, her face dead except for the hatred burning in her eyes. "Just go home, 'Burbs. It's unbelievable you haven't gotten yourself killed yet. Don't talk to me again."

She swiped at her nose, exposing her wrist dotted with tiny puncture wounds. I opened my mouth to say something, but Creed spoke up first.

"Don't worry. We won't bother you anymore. But you know where we are."

"Under a bloody bridge by now," she scoffed. "Well, I guess I made the right choice then." She looked over her shoulder, and her entire posture changed—from defiant to broken in one ripple. "Just leave me alone," she whispered. Then the heels clicked again on the pavement, faster and faster until she was across the street and down the block, headed toward the clubs.

Without May, Santos seemed adrift. "She can go screw herself, or Maul or whoever she's doing these days," he said, but that didn't change his haunted expression or the way he started avoiding me and Creed and our newest safe place, which changed almost nightly—under the University Bridge or the trestle, tucked behind old brownstone apartments. We had a plastic tablecloth Santos stole from some restaurant on Broadway, plus the latest issues of *The Stranger* or *Seattle Weekly* to shield us from the cold until we could find something permanent.

One night Creed and I shivered under the Olive Street bridge. I unzipped the potato coat and his coat from New Ho's and slipped my arms around his ribs—thinner now than ever. He had begun coughing, too.

I put my lips close to his ear, hoping my breath would warm him. "From the beginning, you kept telling me to go home. What do you think now?"

"I still think you should go home. If I could, I would take you there myself. It has to be better than here."

My old life seemed so far away—everything that was here, now, had taken over. That girl I was then, Joy, didn't exist anymore. Was Creed's reason for being on the street any better than mine?

"What about you?" I asked huskily, taking small breaths to avoid another cough. "Why don't you go home?"

Creed pulled me closer to him so our coats closed around us like blankets. Our faces were touching, forehead to forehead, almost making everything around us disappear under this tent of plastic and newspaper and hair and breath.

"I've thought about it," he said. "I could go home and live with that *asshole* and my mom and everything would go back to how it was before, and I would probably go off to school and play in my spare time until I ended up an asshole, too, who plays guitar in cafés on the weekends and beats up his wife for kicks. Then someday I could have a little kid to kick around and treat like shit who can grow up to be just like me."

He stopped. Held his breath, and I held mine. Underneath the coats, our hearts were pounding together with the same wild rhythm as the traffic vibrating overhead.

"Or."

"Or what?" I whispered. His words tickled my lips.

"Or . . . I could stay here and change everything. With you."

That's when it happened.

Everything and nothing like I'd imagined—like that first time I saw him and the future all rolled into his flesh against my flesh, lower lip, upper lip, skin, tongue, all together and urgent and searching and deep and going where we had never gone before.

His hands ran through my hair, smoothing over my skin

and the lobes of my ears while I touched him, face and neck and hair, all the places I had been waiting to see, to feel, to taste. I could feel him letting go of the thing he carried with him, stringing him tightly to his past the same way I was strung to mine. He was no longer trying to protect me—even from himself.

We were both letting all of it release, like balloons into the sky, popping like the kisses he gave me again and again and again.

Under the bridge, traffic above us and coats around us, hearts thudding with the steady perfection of this moment, I thought of every word I had never before dared to think about him.

Future. Hope.

And love, as the rain slowed to a misty trickle through the long and beautiful night.

32

After that night, everything about being here, being on the street, fell into place. Maybe we were sleeping under bridges and behind Dumpsters. Maybe we were freezing and my lungs were getting worse, but I could feel my layers of protection falling away.

Creed was different too. Kissing me had brought down the final wall he'd kept between us. As we became more entwined, I could no longer hide the words that were burned into my flesh just months ago, even though it was an entire lifetime away.

ASHES.

He discovered it first with his fingers. He gently traced the letters, now pink against the backdrop of my skin tone as I held my breath, waiting for him to pass judgment.

And then.

And then, he kissed them, each letter softer than the last, until every scar had been touched by him.

I let him believe that someone did this to me because it was too painful to tell him the truth.

He didn't ask me where they'd come from, only said, "There are scars you can see, and the ones you can't. I knew you had them, Triste."

Then he gathered me into his arms, and I cried.

I woke to Creed's cheek pressed against mine, bodies entangled and warm amid clothes and coats. It was Saturday. We knew what we had to do.

On the weekends, we haunted the club scene—Neumos, Chop Suey, even the old Crocodile Café, a legendary club that had launched a bunch of Seattle bands before it closed and then recently started back up. Creed could get a gig striking the band equipment here and there, and when he was really lucky, the club let him fill in for someone. The word on the street was that Creed could fake his way through any song after only a few notes—like my friends muddling through Rock Band songs to unlock the next batch, but for real.

I hid in the shadows of the clubs, afraid of seeing Asher again and yet desperate to know if he had done something to Neeta.

We ran into Santos, all oozing excitement, at the Croc. "Hey," he said excitedly, "have you found somewhere to crash for Halloween? I heard there's gonna be this huge party down in the warehouse district—some rented space with a DJ and bands. Maybe we can sneak in—Creed, you got any contacts?"

Halloween. These days store windows along Broadway had everything from red afros to bondage in the windows— Christmas for freaks and weirdoes. It hadn't even crossed my mind, except the wetter and colder it got outside, the crazier Capitol Hill would get and the more dangerous life would be for me. Santos had gotten me more drugs, but I didn't know if that would be enough to stave off bronchitis, or worse, pneumonia.

During the day, Creed gathered intelligence and scoped out the scene while I spainged for a few bucks to get us food until the next gig—a house party, where we could crash for the night, or one of the club trailers, with cushions holey and permeated but a thousand times better than sleeping in the rain. Weeks passed this way.

Santos came with us sometimes, but mostly he found somewhere else to crash. "You guys go ahead," he told us one night. "I'm going to the shelter."

Creed said nothing, only watched him darkly.

"What?" Santos shouted. "Don't fucking look at me like that. I'm outta here." He shoved his hand in his pocket, and a small packet, a hot pink square, came tumbling out.

I picked it up and read the slogan: *Protect America. www.plannedparenthood.com.* I blushed a little thinking about Creed—kisses and skin and closeness, yet still innocent. He hadn't pressured me at all. Nothing like Asher.

Santos snatched it out of my hand, and I grinned. "So that's it?" I teased. "That's why you haven't been hanging around us? You have a girlfriend? What about May?"

I remembered the way she looked, the last time we'd seen her. Thin and strung out, but dressed to the nines. She'd abandoned our family. Blood was thicker than sex—or at least, I'd thought it was.

Creed's eyes locked with mine, as if he was giving me a warning.

Santos wouldn't look at either one of us. "Yeah. That's it. Just don't tell May, okay? 'Cause we're kinda . . . fuck it. I'm outta here."

Creed and I cruised around on Broadway for a couple of free coffees and day-old Starbucks lemon bread, my favorite on the street or not, and we trudged down toward Chop Suey to check out their lineup. Gravity Echo, Universal Hall Pass, Symbion Project.

Since the weather had turned, social services and church people were out in full force with toiletries and food packs, scarves and those lame stretchy gloves. Saturdays were the best—there was always somebody giving out water bottles and cans of tuna. When he still lived at home, Jesse would have been among them.

"I'm gonna go up to the college and see if I can sneak into the showers," I told Creed, taking a huge bite of my lemon bread.

Some crumbs landed on my lip, and he kissed them away.

"Yeah. Just stay out of Maul's way, okay?"

I nodded.

"Hey, I saw some people giving out socks and soap up there—maybe you could stop by and get us some? Big group. Church kids or something—they looked pretty straight edge."

I narrowed my eyes and took another bite. "Yeah, like you're not. You act all tough, but underneath I know *exactly* what you're about."

"Oh yeah? What's that?"

The same thing he'd always been about, since the moment I first saw him. The thought of it flustered me, how much I trusted him.

"Well," I responded, "right now you're all about getting the Croc gig. So break a leg."

I headed toward the school, bundled in the potato coat, which had now taken on a blackish-grey sheen. I suppressed a cough, knowing what it meant. It would start with bronchitis, and eventually it would become much more.

The thought of approaching the group terrified me. My brother wouldn't be with them, but there was still the possibility one of his old friends would recognize me. I'd never mastered quickness like Santos, or disguise like May, but I had to try.

A police car zoomed around the corner, sirens blaring. Cops clumped around the youth group.

"He's got her backpack!" a boy shouted. He must have been one of them, because the cops were actually listening.

A homeless guy had fallen to the ground, rolling around and shouting, "I don't know nuthin'! Leave me alone!"

People were looking at him—normals and street people and cops and everyone—so no one paid any attention to me, a ghost girl weaving among them. There was a familiar smell of sweat and urine and some unidentifiable combination of chemicals and rot.

As I got closer, I realized who it was: Stench, splayed on the sidewalk and surrounded by cops. With my backpack clutched in his arms. The little Lego driver tumbled out and split in two. The boy kept shouting as normals and street people looked on with interest.

I knew that voice. It was the last voice I expected.

What was he doing here? What was he doing home from Western?

J1.

My brother Jesse.

33

Jesse, who was supposed to be two hours north of here, stood only a few feet away.

Waves of who I was crashed against the undertow of who I'd been, swirling in a heady vortex. Would he notice me? Would I be invisible to someone who had known me since birth? Should I run? And what was he doing here now, after he'd turned me away when I needed him most?

If I had been alive and present, I would have used my street power to disappear. But I was frozen, fused to a spot in the concrete, with Stench's shout a muted rumble in my ears. The cops started shooing everyone away. "Step back, give us some room here."

One of the cops held his knee in Stench's back, pinning

him to the ground. He flailed wildly until the cop clipped his wrists into a pair of handcuffs. Another cop was trying to calm my brother, who was shouting in a hoarse voice, "Where's my sister? What have you done with my sister?" Everyone watched, spellbound, as more sirens joined the cacophonous whine.

Through the crowd, I spotted the one person who wasn't looking at my brother or Stench.

Santos. He was looking directly at me.

A wild thought flashed through my head—he'd been there, hadn't he, when the cop first searched the streets with my junior-class picture? Joy's picture, which looked nothing like me anymore. Did Santos know? Had he been keeping my secret all this time?

The cops took Stench in one car and my brother in another. Now that Jesse had calmed down a little, he was on his cell phone, probably calling our parents. My own phone was hidden away. Even Creed hadn't discovered it in our new and frantic explorations of each other.

The crowd dispersed, leaving only Santos and me. I could see it in his eyes—hurt, disappointment, shame. I was back to 'Burbs, the runaway who didn't belong here with Creed or any of the rest of them. My story meant nothing compared to what they had been through. I knew it, and he probably did, too.

But I still wanted a chance to explain. I held his gaze as I walked toward him. "Santos."

He didn't respond.

"Santos, I—"

"Whatever it is, you shouldn't tell me," he said.

"But wait," I said desperately. What would I tell him? "You should know—"

"I told you, I don't want to know. Things aren't always how they look. We're family, that's the only important thing."

"Even though we're not together anymore? Even though we don't even have a safe place to sleep and May is with Maul? Even though every time you disappear and come back, there's a little bit less of you, and I don't even know why?"

Santos didn't speak for a moment, only stared at me like he'd already vacated a long time ago.

"We all have our secrets," he said. "You'd better find Creed before yours get a lot worse."

Santos was right. It did get worse.

Suddenly the entire neighborhood was swarming with police posting my picture and questioning anyone on the street. Had they seen this girl? Had they seen her with a homeless man?

Joy's picture—my picture—ended up on the front page of the *Seattle Times* in every newspaper vending machine from here to the Eastside.

NEW INFORMATION ON DISAPPEARANCE OF ISSAQUAH GIRL
New information has surfaced in the case of Joy Delamere,

17, who disappeared from her Issaquah home over two months ago on August 17.

Her mother and father, Peter and Elena Delamere, both work in the financial industry—she as a financial planner and he as a nonprofit donations consultant employed by Valen Ventures, owned by local mogul Steven Valen. After Valen's son, a friend of the girl, was cleared of involvement, it was believed she may have been kidnapped for ransom due to her parents' connections with top-level Seattle wealth.

However, new evidence has come to light linking her disappearance to the homeless population in the Capitol Hill district of Seattle. Experts estimate up to a quarter of the neighborhood's population are sex offenders, including a suspect who has been taken into custody. The girl's eagle-eyed brother, Jesse Delamere, 19, spotted her backpack in the homeless man's possession, prompting further police investigation.

A piece of jewelry belonging to the girl was already recovered from a pawn shop in downtown Seattle. The owner, Alyana Ivanova, stated she was certain she had not seen the suspect in connection with the item. "I turn away stolen items all the time," Ms. Ivanova said. "Though it is impossible to recognize everyone."

Mayor Marcus Ballentine, for whom the tent city population Marcusville was named, said in a statement, "We are doing everything we can to restore the girl to her family as safely and quickly as possible."

★ ★ ★

The rest of the story folded into the vending machine, but the picture taunted me from every street corner.

The neighborhood was operating on a heightened sense of excitement as the Capitol Hill Halloween Bash grew closer. Everyone in the Seattle music scene would be there— musicians, bands, groupies, a couple of radio stations, and the multitude of indie record labels Seattle was known for, which was why Creed was so excited. He had an official gig as a roadie and might have a chance to do a couple of songs on his own.

Creed and I huddled under the park bleachers in the pouring rain. If he'd noticed me withdrawing when the police scoured Capitol Hill, he said nothing. Only waited patiently, with as much sweetness as the kisses he now bestowed on me with abandon. We munched on day-old pastries we found in the Starbucks Dumpster—pumpkin currant. Not my favorite, but I wasn't about to complain.

"May will probably come," Creed said.

"Why do you care if she'll be there?" I demanded. "She abandoned *us*, remember?"

"She was trying to save us."

"Right." I didn't want to hear about May's sacrifice. "And that's why she stays with him and takes his drugs and practically spits on your shoe every time she sees you? She was playing you for sympathy all that time, getting you to be the big protector until she found somebody better. I can't believe you didn't see it." I stuffed more of the muffin in my mouth.

Creed wiped a drop of rain away from my cheek. "What's going on with you? You've been acting like a stranger lately." He kissed me softly, and I hoped he couldn't hear the rattle in my lungs, increasing every day. "Are you okay?"

No. I was anything *but* okay. It was becoming more and more clear my days were numbered—days of making it through the fall without getting sick, of leaving the past behind me, of leaving Asher. Of any kind of future with Creed.

A light suddenly dawned in his eyes. "You're jealous. You're jealous of May."

"No, I'm not." I couldn't look him in the eye as I said it. So maybe I was jealous, even if that was only a tiny drop in the ocean that threatened to drown me. "I can't understand why you want to stick with her when she totally abandoned us—I mean, you and Santos. You talk about family—"

"If you think there's something going on between me and May, then you don't know anything about me."

"That's not what I meant."

"What *did* you mean?"

What could I say—that I wanted him to want to protect me and only me? I knew it wasn't fair. It wasn't who Creed was, but it didn't stop me from longing for it. I could sense him straining against my expectations, like that horse in the ocean. It turned a key in me, a muted click only I could feel.

"Maybe May was right," I said softly. "If you're such a protector, then why didn't you protect your mom?"

The second I said it, I regretted it. What was a key in me

was a knife in him. The closeness I had felt from him just moments ago withdrew, leaving a vacuum. His blue eyes went stormy. The soul of him, written right there on his face for me since the first time I'd seen him in the darkness of the club, recoiled and retreated into the locked chamber of his heart.

"Creed, I'm sorry. I didn't mean—"

But it was too late. He was already backing away from me, in body and in spirit. "You don't know anything about my mother. Or May. Or me. Nothing."

34

The night of the Halloween party, everyone from the normals to the most strung-out hipsters jammed into an abandoned warehouse building for what was sure to be an epic party.

They took IDs and cover at the door, but Creed had a backstage pass—he was handling equipment for all three bands taking the stage, if you could call it that. Plywood sheets scattered across some crumbling concrete blocks, with a tangle of cables and extension cords.

Creed dressed in his usual raggedy T-shirt, jeans, and army surplus jacket, though he had borrowed my black eyeliner to complete his look—either zombie or dead rock star. I didn't ask. We weren't talking much since the fight.

I wore a shredded black lace number I'd smuggled out of St. Vincent's under the potato coat. My skin had whitened as my cough wore on, dark circles spreading under my eyes. I could barely keep them open some days.

That night, I tucked an inhaler and my cell phone against my ribs before stashing the coat in a bush. I ran through the rain into a totally different universe—one populated with the manic menagerie of the underground.

A cough caught me off guard and shook me violently. It was cold in here, and then hot, with not enough air for the hundreds of people pouring in.

"How do I look?" Santos appeared in a shiny pleather skirt and bustier with a weird, enormous thrift-store necklace, fishnets, and heels. I had to do a double take. He almost looked like May, except without the track marks and haunted pallor. He wore heavy makeup—lashes long and exaggerated, lips the color of dried blood. Actually, he made a prettier girl than May.

"You look hot, actually."

Santos grinned. "Yeah?"

I giggled. "Yeah. You make a pretty smokin' girl."

Santos grabbed my shoulders and planted a crazy kiss on my lips. "You, too, beautiful. You know I love you. Oh, that reminds me." He dug into his pocket and pressed a half-full bottle of amoxicillin in my hand. "Hard to get this time—sorry it took me so long."

I silently offered a prayer of thanks. This would keep the

floodwaters in my lungs at bay just a little while longer, until I figured out what to do next.

When Santos disappeared back into the crowd, I touched my lips and came away with a streak of red on my fingers. My skin still tingled, like in that kiss there had been some kind of farewell. A surge of missing came up in my chest—missing the squat house. Missing Santos coming up the stairs in the middle of the night and cuddling in a puppy pile with May and Faulkner. Missing the simple kindness of coffee made from old grounds. Missing Creed.

The DJ worked magic on the crowd, first lulling them with hypnotic beats, then tearing them up with gut-wrenching guitar riffs. It seemed like everyone under the age of twenty-five was here, sweating and kissing and throbbing into this twisted night. It was illegal to smoke in restaurants and public buildings in Seattle, but in this dingy warehouse the lights bounced off a choke of haze.

At first I thought Creed didn't see me, he was so focused on his job. But then he spotted me in the outer rings of the pit. He nodded, then went back to his work.

The first band took the stage late, ripping through their instruments in typical Seattle indie style. No one batted an eyelash when I found my way over to the keg and scored a free beer. Creed didn't drink, which made me want a cold draft all the more. He leaned against the wall behind the stage, closing his eyes like he was listening to a lullaby.

Even if the music sounded like it came out of a garage, maybe he could hear the hidden beauty of it, woven among the notes. I took the last swig of my beer and refilled it at the tap.

Santos was working the crowd, laughing and talking to a thick figure in full bondage getup. My eyes kept wandering back to him in his costume. He looked as much like a real girl as May or me and nothing like the naked boy I remembered from the pool, bare and as dear to me as any of my own brothers.

That seemed so long ago now. That was the night I'd first lied to them, and I'd been lying ever since.

At last the band ended their set. Creed sprang into action, a tall shape moving in the darkness. The DJ went back to the pulsing techno.

I weaved my way back among the bodies, watching for allies and enemies as I went. Some guy in a creepy clown getup grabbed my ass. "What'll you do for twenty bucks?" he asked with a leering grin.

What would May have said, now that she had given all of her powers to Maul? I ignored him and pushed past with my beer in hand.

Creed frowned when he saw me. He looked out over the sea of heads. "May's here," he shouted through the throng of sound. "Maybe you can find her and see if she's okay."

I stared at him. A retort died on my lips. For Creed, checking on May was only that: checking on her, nothing more.

I suddenly felt ashamed for ever thinking anything else. I would tell him, as soon as the party was over. Maybe I would tell him the truth . . . about everything.

For now, I just nodded.

The second band started up, ramping the music to the next level. Neeta would have loved it. She'd be hovering around the merch table as soon as the show was over, chatting easily with the band. The table, piled with T-shirts, CDs, and buttons, was guarded by a werewolf and some kind of mutant punk video-game monster ready to put up a fight if someone like Santos tried to filch a sticker.

Creed talked in low shouts with one of the organizers—the band was cutting their set short because of some argument between the lead and drums. I tried to catch Santos's eye, but he'd disappeared. The bondage guy he'd been talking to was nowhere to be seen.

I slipped around the edges of the smoky horde, the room spinning a little as I went. Noise from the string of giant speakers filled the space where warm, weirdly costumed bodies didn't.

No one noticed a skeletal girl in a slip as she staggered back and forth, grinning a bloody grin before letting her strap fall down one shoulder and pushing against one guy, then another.

Nobody except me.

May saw me watching and dropped the grin. "What the fuck do you want?" She gently laid a kiss on the shoulder of a buff tattoo guy and mouthed the words *Be right back.*

As she teetered closer to me, I could smell a stench on her breath like an open grave. She looked around, but it was impossible to recognize anyone in the pounding sound and darkness. Maul could be everywhere and nowhere, like God or the devil. It didn't matter if he was actually watching, as long as we felt like he was. Just like Asher.

I caught her against me. "May—"

But she cut me off in a high, frantic voice. "You're gonna get me killed, 'Burbs. Don't you get it? Maul is gonna fucking *kill* me, and all you want is to soothe your conscience. Just stay the hell away from me!"

Tattoo Guy stepped in closer and put his arm around May, scowling in my direction. "You okay? I don't wanna get involved in some cat fight."

May reeled and nearly fell down. "Back off," she sputtered. "I'm gonna need a fix after this."

"May, don't. Please." It was so hot in here. My breaths came out in short, painful puffs.

"*Please.* You have such goddamn nice manners, 'Burbs. You and Creed can go take care of each other off in the sunset while me and Santos fall off the edge of the fucking planet. It'll be so much easier for you then." She turned to Tattoo Guy with a ghostly smile. "C'mon, let's get outta here. You got something to ease my pain, or do I have to move on?"

"Yeah, I got something." He reached into his pocket and flashed a bag of white.

"May?"

But she wasn't paying attention to me anymore, only the carrot dangled in front of her and whatever she hoped to bring back for Maul. Invisible or not, I had failed.

35

Creed stood in the darkness with an electric guitar, practicing for the moment he'd get to take the stage. He didn't need to hear about May now—or about the drugs. I would tell him everything later, after he'd had one moment to shine.

As the beer flowed more plentifully and money and various substances exchanged hands, the crowd worked into a frenzy waiting for the headliners, Gravity Echo, and their new breakout hit "Countdown to Fate." There were the die-hards, the ones who knew Gravity Echo had started in a trailer and played grungy house parties and the Croc long before they played Neumos, Chop Suey, and then the Showbox, the pinnacle venue for Seattle bands. Then there were the groupies who'd just discovered "Countdown to Fate" after widespread airplay and an MTV spot, and who were suddenly obsessed with the front man's bed head and the drummer's drink of choice (Tanqueray and tonic, I knew from Neeta).

I stood on tiptoes to see if Santos had come back, but I couldn't see him. Everything—the lights, the faces, the stage—had become blurry and bright.

"Please, let Creed be great," I whispered. There were music people here. Recording labels. Radio stations. One word from any of them, and he could live out his dream.

Where would that leave me? There were street powers, but not for me. What I needed were concrete survival skills, and I had none.

Weird images popped into my head—of the church lady with the potato coat and a fistful of soup and cookies. Of the New Ho's guy with the zigzagging eye. Creed and Santos trusted him. They had skills, living close to the ground, but not on the streets. Was that even possible for me? Was there somewhere in the middle I was missing?

The crowd thrashed, high on things natural and unnatural, as the second band finished its last song. The guy Creed had been talking to took the stage and screamed out, "Babel Sky, everybody! Give it up for Babel Sky!"

A cheer rose on the heels of smoke and ash, and a cold ripple ran through me again. A bead of sweat rolled into my eye, reminding me of the blood that had dripped down my face when Maul hit me.

The band started packing up their equipment with Creed's

help. The drummer stayed behind and the bassist lingered, waiting to see what was going to happen, if the equipment boy had more mettle than winding cords and hauling gear.

Then the emcee shouted over the crowd, "Now I've got something totally different for you—a local guy who's been part of the music scene for a long time, even though you've never heard of him. This guy is going to go places, people. So pay attention and remember the name: *Street Creed*. You first heard it here, motherfuckeeeers!"

Creed was alone on the stage while the entire room—five hundred people, maybe more—held their collective breath to see if this tall, skinny kid had something to say that no one had heard before. He was grubby as hell with his hair hanging in his face, but his eyes shone like light piercing darkness. I could barely listen because I was trying to swallow the closure in my throat.

Creed stood there, taking it all in. I started to get nervous for him. Any second now, the crowd would let out the breath of air in a groan, and he would miss his chance to dazzle this dangerous, electric mass. The sound system screeched, sending a ripple through the audience.

Then his eyes landed on me, and he smiled.

"Triste." His voice sounded like a whisper, reminding me of the first time he'd ever said my name. "This is for you."

Creed laid into the borrowed electric guitar with the fierce vulnerability I had seen when we were closest, and now he had invited five hundred people in. The exhale of the crowd never came, only a gasp—deeper and deeper as they realized what they were a part of. Something true and fresh and entirely new.

And then he started to sing.

Even I couldn't anticipate the rawness of his voice or the way he could spellbind an audience, though I'd heard him play on the street and sing to me, alone on the mattress of the squat house. He sang about the color of skin, and of longing, and of dust falling. He sang of kisses and ashes.

He was singing about us.

When he finished, they cried out for another. Creed hid a smile, as if he'd been waiting for this—hundreds of people, all of them waiting to hear what would come out of him next.

I wanted to know for the rest of my life.

The music hypnotized me, exhilarated me, choked me, and let me breathe again all in the same phrase. He was rough and then gentle, intimate and untouchable. It gave me a chill to know I knew him. I belonged here, with him.

One second I couldn't feel my body, and the next someone was clutching my shoulder roughly, nails digging into my flesh and spinning me into the darkness of the crowd.

There stood May, as if a tomb had swallowed her up and spit her back out.

"Trissssste, you gotta come with me," she slurred, spittle gathering at the corner of her mouth.

Creed's voice tripped, but he kept singing. Had he lost me in the crowd? The thought made me dizzy.

"May, what are you doing here? Just . . ."

"No, lissen. Yougotta . . . juss . . . now." Her demands came out in halting, hazy speech.

She staggered a little and caught herself against a Stormtrooper, who coldly removed her from his arm and went back to watching Creed—exactly what I wanted to do.

"You're high," I spat. "Just go find Maul or whoever you're seducing now and just let me—"

"You donunderstannn . . . Something happen . . . you gotta come. Please." She clutched my shoulder again with surprising strength. "Get Creed, too."

The anger was pumping in my veins where Creed's words had been just a moment ago, and I felt the loss of them acutely. "In case you hadn't realized, he's up onstage playing his music for this entire crowd. You picked the wrong friends. So no, I don't think I'll be going with you right now."

"Pipe down," growled the Stormtrooper. "Take it somewhere else."

I wiped the sweat from my forehead. It was so cold in here all of a sudden.

May wasn't letting go—she was digging in deeper and pulling me toward the door. "Please! Sssss . . . antossss! You gotta come!"

The room lurched to a stop and made me want to throw up. "Santos? What happened?"

"You gotta come. L-l-l-lot of blood."

Santos. Oh, God. The bondage figure, and Santos rocking

his tight skirt and bustier before disappearing out of the throng, flashed through my head.

I followed May, determined to get through. She tripped and splattered onto the concrete amid a circle of dark figures who stepped back to avoid her fall. I helped her to her feet, feeling more and more desperate. I couldn't hear Creed's music anymore, only the pounding of my eardrums.

Santos.

Blood.

May lurched outside and into the network of alleys connecting the warehouse district.

A small, furry figure darted across our path, dotted with gravel and murky puddles. Pallets and rotting furniture littered the way. I shivered in the cold and wished I had the potato coat now. Any second it might start raining again, and I was almost naked in the shredded black dress.

May dragged me behind a reeking trash heap to where a figure lay on the ground.

I didn't recognize the face. It was beaten so badly that even in the darkness, I could see where bones met bones and crushed skin opened into a pool of black. The body was crumpled—skin bruised and torn in unnatural directions.

But the worst was the mouth. Lips were cracked and teeth broken where no words could save them, no matter how fast or furiously they streamed.

I knew that skirt, those legs, ending in a pair of shabby red pumps.

A sob escaped, and I realized it was mine. And May's, too.

"We have to get Creed," she choked out. "We have to get him we hafff to get him*imim*." Her words disappeared into sobs. "I'll go back, I'll get him. You stay here. Maybe we can— mmmaybe there's time—can you . . ."

CPR. I knew CPR. Was he still alive? Was there enough of him left to help him start breathing again?

I knelt down and touched his skin. Still warm. There wasn't much of a nose to grab on to. Not much I could do. I put my fingers against his neck, praying, *Please, God, let him be okay.* I pressed against his chest, willing it to move up and down.

May collapsed to the ground.

No one was coming.

Blood leaked out of Santos into an oily puddle and spread like smoke. And then I noticed it.

On the ground next to his feet was a torn-open pink packet and a rolled-out white latex tube, coated with red.

"What happened?" I asked. I didn't want to see it with sudden, terrifying clarity.

I felt tired, so tired. And hot, even though I knew it was freezing, out here in the night.

May turned to me with the fierceness of a cornered animal. "All thisss time you've been judging me, judging all the time, and I'm jusss staying alive—and here's Santos, right under your nose. Where do you—you think he was going? You think you're *sooo* much better than everyone else, 'Burbs. You don' know *shit*."

The words pierced me, not because they were cruel, but because they were true.

Details flashed through my mind, all of them pointing to the same thing—the late nights, the way he seemed broken when he came home, the secrets he was willing to keep. For himself. For me.

Santos knew my secret . . . he'd seen Jesse looking for me. He could die knowing it, and I might never have to lose Creed.

If you're such a protector, why don't you protect your mom?

The words I'd said to him echoed in my mind. I would never have a chance to tell him the truth. He would look out into the crowd, and I would be gone.

But he would have to find out. Santos was dying. There was only one thing I could do.

I pulled out my phone and turned it on.

Sixty-four messages.

One bar left.

I used it to dial 9-1-1.

36

"Joy?"

It was strange to hear her name spoken. It was even more strange to hear it in a voice I'd known since birth. Before birth, even.

"Joy, is that you?"

Instantly I felt like I was six years old, the time I got separated from my family at the zoo, fell down the concrete stairs and hit my head. There'd been blood everywhere, exactly like there was now—only this time it wasn't my blood.

Here was my mom just like on that day—hugging me and holding me tight, filling my nose with the scent of her hair, clean and peachy, and pressing against my skin, dirty and streaked with Santos's blood.

I'd expected to feel numb when I saw my family, not this horrible tearing in two between fear and relief. They drove up behind a police cruiser just as the EMTs wrapped Santos's barely breathing form in blankets. I knew that by saving Santos, I would be returning to captivity.

I didn't expect the tears to fall at seeing my littlest brother again. Jonah jumped out of the car and ran toward me as my parents watched the medics lift Santos's body onto a stretcher.

But one thing I had expected. As the ambulance pulled away with Santos and May by his side, she watched me from the window, her eyes filled with a mixture of envy and hate.

She was right, after all. I was just 'Burbs, a girl from Issaquah, playing at being homeless. I was going back, and she was going to the hospital with Santos, who might not survive.

Both my parents were crying and hugging me—Dad crushing my head against his chest, and Jonah clinging to my waist and almost making me topple. Part of me hated that they were here, and the other part just wanted to let them hug me to sleep.

What are you doing here? What happened? Were you kid-napped? Did you escape? Are you all right? How did they find you? Did anyone hurt you?

The questions kept coming, one on top of the other amid the hugs and smothering and tears. They touched my head and face, to know I was real in front of them.

Not invisible. Maybe I never had been.

My mother gently stroked my hair, the white and

washed-out blue and dark roots, betraying my true identity. "Did *he* do this to you?"

She meant Stench. That's what they thought—that he'd had me all this time. They knew nothing at all about Asher.

She was crying softly, her hands never breaking contact. "Did he . . . how did you . . . did he hurt you?"

"Elena . . ." My dad's voice was a warning.

"I mean . . . you don't have to talk about it right now. Right now you're here, you're safe." She clutched me in her arms.

"She's shivering," my mother called to the police officers.

But it's hot, I thought. Though I didn't have the strength to tell them. My eyes were blurring from heat, then cold.

The cops produced a small silver emergency blanket, nowhere near enough to keep out the chill. My potato coat was down the street, still stuffed into a bush. I must've looked like hell in my shredded black lace dress and streaming eyeliner, ten or fifteen pounds lighter than when I'd left.

"Joy, what happened?" my mother was saying. "Are you all right?"

A sob wouldn't let the words out. I couldn't get enough air for words. Fluid pressed up through the depths, as if I were drowning.

My dad hushed everyone. "Let her alone," he whispered, hugging me tight. "We don't know what she's been through. Let her have a chance to breathe. We can figure everything else out later." He gently pulled Jonah away from me and touched my mom on the shoulder.

"Here, baby, take this." My mom pressed a brand new inhaler with my name, my own name, on it. "I've been keeping all of your meds in the car, just in case we found . . ."

But she couldn't finish her sentence. It was too much, me being here.

The music wafting through the cold night air had shifted dramatically in the last few minutes, signaling the headline band taking the stage, and Creed . . . Creed would be looking for me.

"Wait, I have to go back," I pleaded, pushing the words through the blinding pain that had suddenly enveloped my head.

"What are you talking about?" my mom demanded frantically. She pushed her lips to my head and released. *My God, Peter,* I heard her say. *She's burning up. Look at her skin—she's white as a ghost!*

The cough I'd been holding in burst out of me as I struggled to fill my lungs, which felt like they were full of flood and fire.

Creed wouldn't find me. I would disappear without a trace, with only May to tell him what had happened—if she ever saw him again. Who knew what Maul would do to her now.

"We need to take her to the station," the cop was saying. He tried to step between my parents and me, and my mother turned on him in slow motion.

"Like hell you do," she roared through the waterfall rushing past my ears. "She's not going to the station. She's going to the hospital."

I looked over the scene behind me and captured it like a living photograph—the gravel and garbage strewn all over the alley, the pools of rain and blood, the pounding of the headline band drifting through the air and settling on me like a dew.

Peter, growled my mom, *help me get her in the car so we can take her to the ER.*

But I can't, I said miserably, feeling my knees buckle.

There was no escaping Joy now. Would Asher be waiting for me? Barbed wire tightened in my chest.

Where was Creed?

My dad led me into the car, and I was still looking over his shoulder. Toward the warehouse, where Creed would be looking for me.

I was good at leaving, I'd told him that. I just didn't think I'd be leaving him.

A tall figure emerged from the darkness, warm breath pumping mist into the freezing air and creating a halo of light around his head. *Creed.*

The car door closed with a thud, and my dad got into the front seat. Everyone's eyes followed mine, to where Creed stood in the concrete landscape, his face stricken. With confusion. With betrayal. With hurt.

And maybe a flash of terrible understanding as he watched us drive away.

37

My first memory was the day I stopped breathing.

I was five years old. It was just Jesse and me then. We were supposed to go school shopping for kindergarten, only I'd been sick again, and Mom had been beside me with the nebulizer full of strange-tasting medications that made my tongue numb and my food taste funny.

Only this time it was different. There was the coughing. Coughing I couldn't stop.

I was underwater and everything was a dream—a tired dream, where I could barely suck air and Jesse came in and out of my room to check on me, and I couldn't eat. Couldn't sleep. Then there was only sleep, and I was dreaming again about the pink boots I wanted to wear for my first day of school.

And then I was drowning.

I didn't know where Mom was, or why she hadn't seen the waters rising in my room until I couldn't focus on the letters of my name on the wall: J-O-Y. Like the song, only I couldn't get a breath enough to sing it. My fingers and toes started to tingle and shake.

The letters got dark and my skin so cold.

That's when Jesse found me.

The rest was a nightmare of riding to the hospital in the ambulance, and then tubes and monitors and acrid smells as my parents hovered over my bed.

Jesse whispered in my ear, "I won't let you die. I won't leave you ever again."

That day, everyone made a vow to the gods of the under-world: They would wrap me gently, keep me in a cage, and watch over me as if my life depended on it. They would suf-focate my spirit to save my body, and then hand the keys to Asher, who engraved our vow on a bracelet with a dangling crow.

Only I'd broken their vow, and now the gods were here to claim me.

By the time we got to the emergency room, Mom had already made calls to let them know we were coming. "She's turning blue, Peter! Hurry!"

Dad carried me, wrapped in the silver blanket like an offer-ing. The cop car pulled up behind us at a crazy angle.

They met us at the door with a gurney. I sank gratefully

into the clean whiteness, even as I struggled for air.

The rest I couldn't distinguish between reality and the memory of what had happened when I was five. Doctors rushed in and out of the tiny room, covering my mouth with a mask. It tasted bitter with a hazy steam of drugs.

There were tubes and needles, and a brief suck of oxygen before the coughing started again, deep and wet in my lungs as if I were in my childhood bedroom again and feeling the floodwaters rise.

"She's stopped breathing," my mom said hysterically, and the tingle in my hands and feet spread up my arms and legs. I would have had a panic attack, but I couldn't get enough air to cry out.

"How long has she been like this?" a doctor asked, and my parents had no answer.

"She was kidnapped. The police just found her, tracked by her 9-1-1 call. . . . She's been gone over two months." They were talking over each other when the police officer appeared.

"We don't believe she was kidnapped." The officer.

"What? What about that homeless man?" My mom, angry.

I didn't want to listen. I felt like I was going to throw up. I gasped for air as a nurse prepped me for an IV and stabbed me with another needle.

"He was released this morning, ma'am," said the officer. "Your daughter has been living on the streets for several months now . . ."

"Can you people take this outside?" It was the doctor, with

a deep and commanding voice. He was tall and lean, like Creed. Maybe he could save me, if it wasn't too late.

My lungs wheezed and crackled as I sank into the river of drugs, brought out of the dream state long enough to cough as though my ribs would break. I felt like I'd been lifted up by the hands of the party crowd and then slammed into the concrete with a vicious thud. *Light as a feather, free as a bird.* Then I was falling, until I hit the bottom like the shattering of glass.

I strained to hear my parents and the officer outside. He was saying something about an AMBER Alert.

There was an AMBER Alert? When did that happen?

That's what I'd wanted, for them to believe I'd been kidnapped. They might still, if I hadn't called to save Santos. He could be in this same ER, only a few rooms away.

"She's been living with a gang of homeless runaways."

Did he mean Creed and Santos and May? "They're not a gang," I tried to whisper, but the doctor didn't seem to be listening. He was hooking me up to some other monitor while a nurse put a tube down my throat.

"One of them is a known drug addict and prostitute with a homeless mother dealing in the U District . . ."

May.

"One of them prostitutes himself outside of clubs, has been kicked out of the foster system, and has been arrested for petty theft and burglary . . ."

Santos.

"One of them doesn't have a record, but we believe him to

266

be a protector who is pimping out the girls in his circle . . ."

Creed? No! It wasn't like that.

"I suggest you have your daughter tested for drugs and STDs . . . any number of things she could have picked up while working the streets . . ."

No. I moaned, but I couldn't get the word past the tube, which was making my throat go into convulsions.

"Shhhhh," the nurse said. "Rest now." She added something to the IV, and in just a few seconds, I was spiraling into darkness.

38

Days and nights passed like dreams—or nightmares, depending on where I was in the cycle of drugs, or coughing, or fighting against my airways, full of water and yet dry as crackling glass.

I don't like what you did last night, Joy, Asher said to me as I slept. *We're going to have to fix it.*

I gasped for air, sending the oxygen monitor into an insistent beeping.

Someone pushed a mask onto my face, tinged with the bitter taste of medicine. I was five again, when this vortex of family terror had officially begun. Perhaps it would end here, as we all faced our worst fear together.

If I didn't die, I would have to face Asher.

Through the web of illness, a familiar sound made the hairs on my neck stand on end. A rumble. The distinctive roar of a DeLorean, as if Asher were outside this hospital room, waiting for me.

Was he here already? Would my parents let him in? But I'd heard them say no one could see me, only my family. It couldn't be.

I opened my eyes to see a sliver of light dart across the wall, a rare moment when I didn't sense another presence in the room—my mom or dad, or the hospital staff poking or nebulizing or checking my X-rays.

I crept to the window, expecting to see the low, silvery shadow of Asher's car in the moonlight, my options flashing before my eyes like I was about to die. But there was nothing but bushes under the window, bathed in the pale glow of clouds.

A nurse came in one morning and started questioning me through the haze.

Was I involved with Asher Valen? Was I living with prostitutes on the street? How did I survive so long out there if my asthma was so severe?

I coughed in response. Why was she asking me these things? Where was my mom?

Another nurse came in to check on me and roared at the other nurse. *I told you and the rest of the press to stay out of here! I'm calling security. . . .*

The press. *Oh, God.*

If I could hide here forever, I thought fleetingly, reality would not come crashing down.

But then I got better.

My parents were still by my bedside at every waking moment as my pneumonia turned a corner. I was still weak, like I had fallen three stories and broken every bone in my body. Every muscle ached.

I'd been changed into a hospital gown. The scar . . . someone would have seen it. My mother? No. She still believed I'd been kidnapped, despite all evidence to the contrary. She couldn't get her mind around the truth. "They're going to catch this criminal," she'd whispered.

I was in a private room now, rarely alone except at night, when my parents went home to take care of Jonah, and I was under the watchful glare of the night staff. They had begun letting me take short walks to rebuild my strength. And that's when I managed to slip out.

Memories of Santos that night echoed in my mind—he had to be in intensive care, if he was still alive. The hallway to the ICU wound down a long corridor and through several sets of white doors. Metal signs instructed us to cover our coughs and wash hands thoroughly to prevent spread of infection.

I found the ICU waiting room, an open space with chairs, a fish tank, and one lone girl. Her thin, broken figure waited in a corner, huddled around a pillow. Her hair spiked every which way, and she looked brittle as a twig.

May.

I don't know why I hadn't expected her to be here, or that my identity as Joy and my identity as Triste might someday collide. Who would I be now?

May looked up, eyes streaked with black and sleeplessness, and maybe withdrawal. She looked fully present, nothing like the last night I'd seen her. She concentrated her full venom on me.

"Get out of my face, 'Burbs. You don't belong here."

May didn't seem to notice that I was wearing a hospital robe myself.

"I came to see how Santos is doing."

"You're a little late," May spat. "He's already been here a week."

"I know." But she had no idea I'd just spent a week here, too. "Is he better?"

"If you can call a coma better, then yeah. They're in there rearranging his face, but at least he's not dead. They said he's gonna be here for at least another month, and then who the hell knows. But his life is pretty much over, thanks to you."

The walls waved a little in the direction of my stomach. "I'm the one who called 9-1-1—how can this be my fault?"

"You're kidding me, right? Juvie? Foster care? The suck-hole who did this to him? Wherever he goes, he's fucked."

I thought I was saving him, calling 9-1-1. I didn't know what to think now—but May was right. A coma was better than dead.

"Creed's gonna be heartbroken—not that he isn't already."

"Creed? Heartbroken?"

May choked on a laugh and coughed wildly, as if she were the one with pneumonia. "What did you expect? You faked us all out, you lied to us, and then you get into a police car and go back home to your warm, cushy house. Was it some kind of experiment? See if you could hack it? Well, looks like you can't. I never should have tried to save your ass—not when you were going to run home to Mommy and Daddy."

The old anger bubbled up, the same feeling I had every time she talked about herself and how she would kill herself if she looked like me. She would kill herself if she'd been a 'Burbs girl. She would kill herself before going to see her mom. She valued May about as much as I valued Joy, which was not at all.

"The ass you should be saving is your own," I said.

May huffed. "Whatever. I'm dead the second I leave this hospital anyway. As soon as I walk outta here, Maul's gonna kill me."

I understood, perhaps for the first time. I was waiting for the same thing, for Asher to kill me.

"Isn't that what you want?" I asked softly.

"What the fuck are you talking about?"

"I'm talking about you. Every time you talk about yourself, it's all about how much you want to die."

She stared at me, daring me to say more.

"May, it doesn't have to be like that."

"Oh, really? How can it be, 'Burbs? How can it be for someone who's spent their whole life on the streets, with a crack addict for a mom and no dad, and my only real friend is about to kick the can in the next room?" A nurse walking by glanced over, but May didn't seem to care. "The only thing I can do to keep from being him is to screw people for a living, and as soon as I walk out that door, I can't even do that because Maul will be there. I got no one, 'Burbs. So tell me, how can it be for someone like me?"

All of our street powers had gone to hell—they were all in my head. Survival skills, that's what Creed had in his music. Santos could talk his way out of almost anything, until he couldn't save himself. May could control people with her body, until someone gained control of her.

And I—I could hide in plain sight, but I couldn't even hide from myself.

"You think the only thing that's worth anything is your body, but you're wrong, May. What about this?" I pointed to my hair, jagged from her cut and white from her dyes. "What about this?" I pointed to her hair. "What about Creed and Santos? You could disguise anyone. You could disguise yourself, if you wanted to."

She said nothing.

"You don't have to go back to Maul. You don't even have to stay in Seattle. You could go somewhere else."

May looked down, and I wondered if she was preparing

for a fresh assault, gathering her energy. Everything was quiet before a certain storm.

Then a drop fell, a drop I never expected. A tear, falling onto the blue herringbone of her chair.

"But what about my mom? Who would take care of her if I left?"

I felt a thud in my spirit.

I wanted to throw my arms around her and tell her everything was going to be okay. To thank her for the sacrifice she made, even though it meant sacrificing herself. But I couldn't—there was an invisible field between us, no matter how hard I tried to penetrate it.

"What about New Ho's? Ron could help you—they're building that housing above the church parking lot. Or a women's shelter? Or Mary's Place? There has to be somewhere you'd be safe . . ." My voice trailed off as she watched me. May already knew what I refused to believe.

"There's no hope for me, 'Burbs. No matter where I go, no matter what I do, death is always gonna be there, waiting. I might as well meet it halfway."

39

When we got back to the house, it was like a mirage—so huge and light and clean—looming in front of me. It was unreal. Back in my own room, all of my clothes were in the closet, bed made, toiletries arranged as if we had company coming.

The company, I realized, was me.

Now I had fresh air to breathe and an unending supply of hot water and pillows, but my parents watched over my every move. Jonah clung to me like a second skin, afraid I might leave any second and never return.

I watched out the windows for Asher, wondering the same thing. When the phone rang, I jumped. Every engine, every shadow made my scar burn with his proximity. It was just a matter of time.

My mom decided to take time away from work until things stabilized. They were trying to keep up some semblance of normal, even though life was everything but.

"You didn't have to take off work, Mom," I said one day after we dropped Jonah off at preschool.

"What am I supposed to do? Leave you here alone?"

"What do you think I'm going to do?" I knew exactly what I would do. I would go straight to the hospital, find Creed if I could.

My mom stopped at a light, and I instinctively checked the mirrors to see if Asher was following. Did he know I ran away? How long would it be before everyone heard I was back?

"It's not about what you're going to do, Joy. It's about what could happen to you."

She turned to me tenderly and wiped a wisp of hair away from my face. "Don't worry, okay? Things are going to be fine. It's all going to be back to normal pretty soon. I called Jesse. He's coming home."

Jesse arrived that night, even though it was a Wednesday and Thanksgiving was still a week away. If he'd been angry when I showed up on his doorstep with Neeta, right now he was furious.

"Why are you here?" I asked, remembering the last time I'd seen him.

"Isn't it obvious? I'm here to take care of *you*."

He pushed past me up to his old room as Mom greeted

276

him at the stairs. Jonah came racing in from the family room, shouting Jesse's name and leaving a trail of Lego parts.

Jesse was storming around the house, Mom was asking me how I was doing every five minutes, Jonah was on the verge of building a Lego metropolis, and I was curled up in a daze when Dad came home with the news.

"Peter, what's the matter?" Mom asked.

A vein was working in my dad's neck. "I *resigned* from my job today."

"What?"

Asher. Asher did it. My throat started to constrict.

"Jonah, why don't you go up to your room to play with those?" Mom said quietly.

"But I'm not doing anything!" Jonah whined from the living room.

Dad threw today's edition of the *Seattle Times* on the table in front of us. The headline read, LOCAL GIRL WITH VALEN VENTURES TIES FAKES KIDNAPPING—like the runaway bride but worse, since I'd hooked up with a drug dealer, a pimp, a prostitute, and various other characters. They knew I was connected to Asher, even though his father claimed I was only an acquaintance and his son had broken off ties with me long before I ran away.

Asher would know I was home.

"This is wrong," my mother whispered, shaking her head. "That—that man—Jesse found the backpack! We saw the dirt, Peter!" She was almost crying.

My dad growled, "She wasn't *kidnapped*, Elena. Let it go."

"She was in the *hospital*! She almost *died because of that man!*" Tears were streaming down her face and she shoved the paper away. "That's why I called Jesse. Maybe he can come home from Western for the quarter—"

"Hell, no!" Jesse shrieked. "I am not coming home to take care of her!"

"Jesse!" My mom gestured toward Jonah.

But Jesse would not be stopped. "You people need to deal with your problems. You're the parents here."

"You're in denial, Elena!" Dad shouted. "Asher told us what happened."

Oh, God. I didn't want to know what he'd told them. My scar ached at the memory.

Dad kept talking. "When the police were investigating, the first person they went to was Asher. That's how we found out he broke up with you."

"*What?*"

"We thought you were abducted—we didn't want to believe you'd run away because of a breakup . . ."

So that's what he'd told them. That's why he hadn't called. I was too stunned to speak.

Then came a mixed flood of anger and relief—anger that he lied to save his own ass, and relief that maybe it was over. Maybe I hadn't heard his car outside my hospital window, and it was just my imagination. Maybe, if he cut me loose, I could finally be free.

My voice had lowered to a whisper. "It wasn't for the reason you think."

They all turned to me—angry, frightened.

Something shifted, like light that streamed into the bedroom I'd shared with Creed and illuminated the dust particles, imperceptible in the darkness.

I could stay here and change everything, with you.

But I had one chance, here with my family, to tell the truth. There was a window of clarity, a gap, when words might make a difference.

Or one word might.

"Look," I said.

Ashes spread across my hipbone.

And they saw.

The letters were thick and pink and twisted now, but they stood out against my skin.

My parents reeled in confusion.

"You mean this was all about Asher?"

My dad looked back at my mom, suddenly grasping what she'd said.

I was spent, all of me ground into particles like sand. They knew nothing about him, not really. "I was suffocating," I said.

Jesse nodded, as if he understood.

"Did he do that to you?" my dad wanted to know. "Has he been hurting you?" The pain on his face was almost unbearable.

Hurt was such a relative word. Creed had so much hurt, he had to leave his abusive father and let his mother fend for herself. Santos had endured years of hurt, and now he was hanging by a thread. May's own mother had rejected her and May punished herself every time Maul hit her, every time she gave her body again. Had Asher hurt me?

If he'd hit me, that would've been *something*. Something I could point to. Words, words were nothing. But every word he spoke taught me to fear him and his threats, his touch, his constant reminder that he'd rescued me and my family. Like a fairy-tale girl sacrificed to save her father, only in this story the prince turned out to be the beast, who would tear her with his claws from the inside out. He even made the girl wound herself.

Were words enough to count as hurting?

My dad reached over, putting his arms around me, and all at once, I was his little girl again.

"Yeah," I whispered, "Asher hurt me. I mean—he never hit me. He hurt me in other ways. He threatened me . . . threatened Dad's job. And he did other things."

"Did he . . . did he do that to you?" my mom asked.

I felt that familiar fear rise in my chest that ached to keep my own words in. I'd failed when I'd asked Santos where he went at night. My words wouldn't help May when she went back on the street with Maul. Worst of all, my words drove Creed away, only moments before I had abandoned him.

But words had power. I needed to learn to use it.

"I did it," I said. "He made me do it, as punishment. And . . . there was going to be more."

I glanced at Jesse, his eyes filled with sorrow. He knew.

"I never really did like him," Jesse muttered, and I let it go. It was his job to know everything, my big brother.

My mom joined us, and even Jesse put a tentative hand on my back while Jonah ran to throw himself around me. Later we could talk about how they'd been suffocating me, too— how keeping me from dying had kept me from living.

But this was enough, for now.

40

There was something liberating about losing everything. When the worst happens and you still survive, it sets you free from fear. We had no survival skills—we'd spent our lives depending on everyone else—and now it was time to learn them ourselves.

My family adjusted to the new me as I adjusted to my life, old but now new. I had changed, just like Neeta said.

School had already been going on for a couple of months, so I struggled to catch up at home with online classes. I didn't mind so much, because it kept me out of the spotlight as the press inferno and gossip died down.

In the meantime, we weathered the storm.

I might have stayed in the safety of my room forever if

Neeta hadn't called and begged my mom to let me meet her at Starbucks, the one we always used to go to, one night.

My mom hesitated. "But then," she said, "if you can survive on the streets for two months, you can probably handle Starbucks."

I sat at an empty table toward the back of the café—busy, on a school night, full of kids I knew, when I had been that other Joy. An image of Asher and Neeta flashed through my mind, him gripping her arm tightly. Was she fading into him even now?

I watched Neeta approach from the far end of the parking lot and remembered what Asher used to say about her: *annoying, know-it-all desi.* Of anybody, she wouldn't be the type to get involved with someone like him. I could warn her at least, even if we didn't have much of a friendship anymore.

A new haircut framed her face. Asher-approved? He would never let me cut mine, said the long darkness of it made me look taller, slimmer. What would he think of the jagged white bob I wore now?

Neeta spotted me in the corner and navigated the tables and other students. I sat on the window seat, with a pillow and a latte for protection. I pushed the other latte I'd bought toward her—nonfat split shot with a splash of cinnamon, plus whip. Her favorite.

"Hey."

"Hey." She gave me the once-over, though most of me

was hidden by pillows. She moved to hug me, then must have changed her mind.

"You have new hair," I said.

She laughed, the same laugh I'd known since we met. *Light as a feather, free as a bird.* We didn't find out until later that we'd been saying it wrong all along. It was supposed to be "light as a feather, stiff as a board." But we had never said it that way.

I wondered if she remembered trying to catch me when I fell. If I could reach out for her now.

"I think you kinda take the prize for new hair," she sniffed.

We could talk about stupid stuff—school, Ari and Ellerie, how the heck had she been since I ran away from home? But there was only one real question between us now, if I had the courage to ask. "When did you start seeing Asher?"

"Huh?"

"I saw you at Chop Suey with him, a couple of months ago."

She looked at me, dumbfounded. "But . . . wait. You were there?"

I nodded slowly. This wasn't going well. I sounded jealous and mean. What I really wanted was to warn her.

She reverted to her childhood accent, an unconscious thing she hadn't done for years. "The police and everybody thought you'd been kidnapped—there was the mud and the open window, and no warning. Nobody could figure out why you might run away, except Asher. He's the one who thought you would be there. So he asked me if I would come with him.

He thought if I was there, you'd come forward. But you didn't. Why?"

"Oh," I said softly. "He was just using you, then." Of course he was. He would do anything to gain control of the situation. Even use my best friend against me. "So you aren't seeing him?"

"Oh my gosh, no, Joy. Even if he hadn't been your boyfriend, I would *never* go out with him." She made a face. "Besides, I thought . . . he said, after the police started investigating him, he said he'd broken it off . . . and I was glad, because I never thought he was good for you. . . ."

I don't know why I was surprised he would lie to her, too. Everything he ever said or did to me was done in secret.

I hugged the pillows closer around my body, an armor of cotton and silk. "Can I ask you something?"

"Sure."

"When we went to see Jesse . . . when we were driving home . . . you said I was different. What did you mean?"

She swallowed hard, and when she spoke again, the accent had completely vanished. "You changed, when you met Asher."

The words hit me in the gut.

"I mean, it was terrible when you were with him. We were all worried about you—especially when I thought he was doing something to you. I was hoping if I took you to see Jesse, you might find some help. I was just as shocked as you were when he turned you away."

Neeta knew?

"But if it helped you get away from Asher," she continued, "then maybe it's good you left. I thought you ran away, but then everyone said you'd been kidnapped. And then Asher wanted to find you . . ."

"But wait," I said breathlessly. "Wait. How did I change? What did you see?"

Her face concentrated. "I don't know . . . it's hard to explain. I don't know what happened but you weren't . . . you. You shrank, like you were in his shadow or something. But then you seemed so into him. I thought maybe I was wrong."

It gave me chills, hearing the truth from her lips. I knew she'd want to hear the truth from mine.

She took a gulp of her latte. "Hey, I know we need to talk, but I thought you might like to do something fun. Ellerie's invited us over for a little—"

"Rock Band?"

She grinned. "Wanna come?"

Five minutes later, we were maneuvering through the parking lot to find her car. "I had to park practically in *Sammamish*, there's so many cars out tonight," Neeta complained, digging through her purse.

She stopped. "Crap, I think I dropped my keys inside, but the car's right over there. Wait for me?"

I wandered toward her car, looking up at the cloud cover overhead. Not long ago, this would have meant spending the night in a Laundromat or under a bridge with Creed. I'd left him there, and he still didn't know what had happened to me. The ache of it caught in my chest.

A slow, grinding sound of footsteps in the gravel alerted my senses.

"Hello, Joy."

A sick feeling crept into my stomach. *How did he know I would be here?*

"I've missed you."

He came into view and I couldn't help it when my body responded. He was a shadow, a dark vortex ripping my lungs out with fear and some other emotion I had once mistaken for love.

"Asher," I whispered.

And suddenly the parking lot was empty, and Neeta was a million miles away, and he held a leash invisible to everyone but me.

He was coming toward me. His eyes burned me with their intensity. With hate, with desire, with something like sadness.

"I've been trying to call you," he said. I was rooted to the spot, couldn't speak.

He reached up to touch my hair first, then my neck, then ran his finger down the side of my coat until he encircled my wrist. *Little bird.*

"I heard you sold the bracelet. Were you trying to hurt me?"

I closed my eyes, willing him to go away. I remembered the first time he had kissed me, exactly like this. Standing so close, not touching, and then capturing me with one brush of his lips. Oh, how stupid I had been. How stupid I was now, to think he wouldn't come after me.

I'd known he would.

Asher brushed his face up next to mine so that I could feel the hint of stubble, smell his custom scent and his cigarettes. Part of me missed it, being under his spell.

"I wanted you to know," he said softly, "I'm willing to give you another chance—but there's going to be a price. I saw that group you were hanging out with on the streets. I watched you with them, Joy." His breath was hot on my neck. "Maybe they'll have to pay, for taking you away from me."

Creed. Santos. May. I was drowning in the possibilities, so deep that I almost didn't see the light.

But then I did. "The girls I was staying with. Just promise me you'll stay away from them. . . ."

Asher chuckled. "Oh, you know I'm not going to stay away from those girls. You can be sure of that."

"Girl," I said.

"What?"

"There was only one girl," I said, with more confidence. The light grew brighter, my breathing stronger. "You're a liar."

Asher's face fell out of the shadows as he stepped away from me, squinting. "What are you talking about, Joy?"

He didn't have anything over my family, over my dad. He only had something over me.

Neeta waved as she came out of the Starbucks, and it gave me courage. "You're a liar," I said again. "I don't know why I ever listened to you." I yanked my wrist from his grip, and he looked stunned. "Go ahead—ruin my dad's career, if you can. But you have no power over me."

The only power he'd ever had over me was what I gave him. And I was done with being his victim.

Neeta came up with her keys aloft, then stopped when she saw him. "What's going on?" she demanded, in a voice I'd never heard from her before. "Joy?"

"Nothing," I said. "Just some unfinished business, but it's done. Let's go?" She nodded, and I joined her under the streetlamp, the light pooling over us like a baptism.

I didn't have to try to be invisible—not anymore.

41

After that, Asher didn't seek me out again. He would tell everyone he'd already cut the crazy runaway girl loose, and good riddance. Only Neeta and I knew the truth: I had nothing to be ashamed of.

She went to Capitol Hill with me, first to visit Santos and then to look into getting a tattoo.

"Of what?" she asked, after I showed her my scars and told her everything.

"A phoenix," I said. I knew exactly where to put it.

Santos was still in the ICU, but they would be moving him soon. For now, he could have a few visitors.

"Heeey, 'Burbs!" he called to me in a hoarse voice, trying to smile through the bandages on his face and body. I had to hold back tears, seeing him like that. They said some damage would be permanent, and this was only the beginning. "May says it's your fault I'm here—so I guess this means I owe you a coffee, chica. The food here is the shit! They got Jell-O, lasagna . . . you wouldn't believe the chocolate cake they've been layin' on me. Frosting is, like, from paradise. Who's your friend?"

Neeta gave Santos a shy smile, and the parts of his face I could see blushed—blushed! I would never have believed it.

"This is my friend Neeta—she's . . . we've known each other since we were kids."

A look of longing passed through Santos's eyes. Longing, and maybe forgiveness, too. "Friends are like family, you know?" he said softly. "You guys . . . you know, May and Creed . . ."

"I saw May the last time I came, when you were still in pretty bad shape. She okay?"

Santos tried to nod, then winced backward from the pain. "Yeah, she's gonna be all right. When I get outta here, we're gonna take care of each other." He kept talking about the plans in a hopeful voice, but both of us knew better. When he got out, he'd go right back into the system, and from there right back onto the streets. Who knew what would happen to May.

"What about Creed?"

Neeta looked at me sharply. *You have changed, Joy,* she said when I told her everything. *You're not afraid anymore.* I knew I could trust her now.

Santos looked away and wouldn't meet my eyes. "Yeah, he hasn't been around much, not since . . ."

He didn't have to finish the sentence. I could finish it for him—*not since I'd disappeared.*

"He say anything about me?"

Santos shrugged, then moaned again with the effort of it. "Not really. But then he's probably already gone now."

"Gone?"

Of course he would be. How could I expect him to say good-bye when I'd left him with no explanation? "But how could he just leave you?" I demanded.

"I guess he figured I was okay here. He said he had some things he had to do. So he went back to Oregon."

Oregon. So it was finished.

Over the next couple of months, life shifted into the new normal. I went back to school an underground hero and started putting in university applications. I had a lot to say in my essays, after my experience on the streets.

I organized a coat drive at school, getting everyone to practically give the clothes off their backs to take three huge garbage bags to New Ho's. The guy with the glass eye, Ron, accepted the bags with a huge smile on his face and gave me a wandery look. That eye had street powers, I was sure of it. But if he recognized me, he never said anything.

My mom kept working as many hours as she could, and

my dad started looking at other jobs. When we ran out of savings, we'd have to put the house up for sale, but at least we faced our fears head on.

Asher stayed the hell away from me. I kept the hair, a fusion of Triste and Joy, even though no one could do it the way May had. My dark roots grew in so fast that they were always more skunk than punk.

Santos was released from the hospital and disappeared. I hadn't been able to find anything out about May, and I didn't know what I could have done to help her. Still, I never stopped thinking about them.

Or Creed.

One afternoon, Mom answered a call on the house phone. "No, there's no one here by that . . . just a minute."

To me she called, "Joy? There's someone on the phone. I think it might be for you."

I hadn't had this feeling in months—of being exposed and vulnerable—but I felt it now.

"Who is it?"

A second later, "Someone named Joel."

I thundered down the carpeted stairs in my socks. I didn't know anyone named Joel. "You don't think it's Asher . . ."

My mom shrugged. "I don't think so. It didn't sound like him. Someone with a nice voice."

I swallowed to keep mine from shaking as I picked up the phone. "Hello?"

Silence.

"Hello?"

"Triste."

The floor dropped out from beneath me. "Creed."

"Hey."

"Creed, I'm so sorry . . . please, I did it to save Santos, I didn't mean to leave you like that. . . ."

"Triste. It's okay. I called because . . . can you meet me?"

My mom stood by, watching my face go from terrified to broken to hopeful to maybe even ecstatic.

"Yes," I said quickly, then, "No. I mean, wait a second." I put the phone to my stomach. "Mom, can I use the car? Please?"

My mom nodded, giving me a cautious look.

"Yes," I said into the phone. "Yes. Where are you? Where do you want to meet?"

"How about Molly Moon's on Capitol Hill?" It was the site of our first date, where he'd bought me an ice cream cone.

"You're here?" I practically shouted. "You're in Seattle? But I thought . . ."

Creed laughed. "Can you just meet me there?"

A half hour and twenty miles per hour over the speed limit later, I walked around the corner toward Molly Moon's. I kept smoothing my clothes—jeans and a sweater with a coat thrown over the top, my white hair standing out every which way, boots clicking on the wet pavement and sounding exactly like May's had so long ago.

What would he think of me now, cleaned up and minty fresh and wearing enough clothes to keep us warm for an entire year on the streets?

I pushed my way into the shop and hit a cloud of warmth and sugary aroma. I glanced around the room, looking for the Creed I remembered—freckled, suntanned skin, stormy blue eyes, a shock of jagged dark hair.

He wasn't here. And I guess I should have expected it.

Then a boy looked up from the bench—hair combed neatly back, wearing a heavy coat, clean jeans, and a thick dark sweater.

My eyes rested on him, this boy I barely recognized—not until he smiled, stood up, and walked toward me. Wrapped his arms around me, my entire body, and lifted me off of the ground in front of the whole room, in this private world we shared together.

"I missed you," he murmured into my hair, brushing his lips against my ear, my cheek, my mouth. He tasted like cream and Creed, the taste I'd missed more than peanut butter and jelly, sour gummies, and anything else I could imagine.

"I thought you were gone forever," I said between kisses, not caring that people around us were staring and smiling. "I was afraid I'd never see you again, that you were gone to Portland and never coming back."

"Portland? Why Portland?"

"Well, Santos said Oregon, and that's where all the Seattle musicians are going, right? So I thought . . . after I left that night, I was afraid . . ."

Creed laughed, his teeth so white and perfect except for

one tiny chip. Awfully perfect, for a boy who had lived on the streets. He kissed me one more time, then reached for two cups of ice cream waiting for us on the table—one salted caramel, one bubble gum. "Come with me."

The air was crisp and cold outside, but brilliant with blue sky and clouds in the way only a January sky in Seattle could be. We walked arm in arm down Broadway, not quite normals and not quite Ave Rats—we straddled the two worlds, belonging to neither.

Belonging only to each other.

"I did go to Oregon," Creed—Joel—said, "but not to Portland. I went home to Astoria."

A ball of guilt welled itself up inside me as I remembered the angry words I'd spoken before the Halloween party, words I'd never had a chance to take back.

"Creed—Joel?" The name felt strange in my mouth, and I wasn't sure I would ever get used to it. "I didn't have a chance to tell you . . . I'm so sorry. I never should have said what I did about protecting your mom. I had no right—"

We stopped near a group of kids sitting along the building, smoking and calling out for spare change. They couldn't even see us now.

"But you *were* right. That's why I went back."

I took a bite of the ice cream so I wouldn't have to speak.

"But you're not going to believe this—when I got there, my dad was gone. I guess when I left, my mom realized I couldn't protect her forever, and maybe she needed to start protecting herself. So she filed for divorce and a restraining order, and she's moving to Seattle. I'm going back to school—here."

I gasped. Here in Seattle? The wonder of it nearly blew me away. He would be close to me, close to Santos and May . . .

"What about May? I haven't seen her in months, not after she stopped camping out in the hospital waiting room. Have you seen her?"

A mischievous smile played across his lips. "Whatever you said to her must have made an impression—she said, and I quote, 'That fucking 'Burbs seems to think the only way I can save myself is by cutting hair. So I'm proving she's full of shit.'"

I looked at him, amazed. "So where is she now?"

"Well, they finally finished that New Ho's apartment building over behind the community college. We talked to Ron, and she got in as one of the first tenants—earning money by doing hair, and probably bitching about it the entire time. Ron is helping with the paperwork to get Santos emancipated and out of the system. He'll be seventeen in a few months, so he's got a pretty good chance, as long as he stays out of trouble."

We walked along, avoiding puddles and panhandlers, though Creed stopped to dole out some change. The sun peeked out from behind a cloud, transforming the whole street into a sparkling alternate world—one with darkest shadows, but also with glimmers of brightest hope.

"Oh! That's not even the best part. You're not going to believe the best part."

"What?"

"Two words: *Recording. Contract.*"

"From the Halloween party? Oh my gosh, from the Halloween party? They heard you? What happened? I mean, you were amazing that night, but . . ."

My heart suddenly lurched. Wouldn't he want to know why I'd run away in the first place? And I would have to tell him— every lie, and every truth. I would have to tell him about the scars, even though now I knew the truth about them myself.

I hoped . . . I *knew* he would understand.

"Creed, I'm sorry I left you—Santos . . . I had my cell phone all that time and didn't tell you . . . there's so much I need to tell you . . . so much I've held back . . . "

He stopped me with a kiss. "I'm not going anywhere— except right now, we're going somewhere. Together."

We turned a corner toward the old brick church and the new apartment building over the parking lot.

"To see May? She's there now?"

Creed nodded. "We can go, but only if you promise to tell me one thing."

"What's that?"

He swept me up in his arms and held me in his gaze, just like the moment I first saw him—only a block or so from where we were now. We'd experienced a lifetime since then, and we still had a whole one in front of us.

"What?" I laughed. "What do you want to know?"

Creed set my feet back down on the ground.

"I want to know your real name."

I grinned, kissing him crazily and feeling the wild, expansive future in every breath.

"It's Joy. Right now, it's pure Joy."

AFTERWORD

"There comes a point when a runaway decides it's safer to live on the streets than to live at home."

That's what the board president at the real New Horizons told me about homeless teens as I was researching this novel. From that moment on, Joy's story irrevocably changed.

I wish the experiences of May, Santos, Creed, and Joy could never happen—but they can and do every day.

Over 1.6 million youth run away each year in the United States, a great many as a result of emotional or physical abuse. Within seventy-two hours, countless teens on the street have been assaulted. Drugs become a way of coping, and many find themselves exchanging sex for food, shelter, and clothing. As of the writing of this novel, Seattle has one of the highest teen homeless populations in the country, with millions more around the world.

What can you do to help?

Begin in your neighborhood, as Joy does. Look for opportunities to give toiletries and essentials, or volunteer in a teen shelter. If you have a friend in trouble, you may be more important than you know. Encourage your friend to find help. True friendship shines through adversity, and there is hope on the other side.

Find ways to contribute at www.hollycupala.com/hope.